Here

"With an irreverent, tell-it-like-it-is, suburban-mom-assassin narrator, Leslie Langtry's *'Scuse Me While I Kill This Guy* delivers wild and wicked fun."
—Julie Kenner, USA Today Bestselling Author

"Darkly funny and wildly over the top, this mystery answers the burning question, 'Do assassin skills and Girl Scout merit badges mix...' one truly original and wacky novel!"
—RT BOOK REVIEWS

"Those who like dark humor will enjoy a look into the deadliest female assassin and PTA mom's life."
—Parkersburg News

"Mixing a deadly sense of humor and plenty of sexy sizzle, Leslie Langtry creates a brilliantly original, laughter-rich mix of contemporary romance and suspense in *'Scuse Me While I Kill This Guy.*"
—Chicago Tribune

"The beleaguered soccer mom assassin concept is a winner, and Langtry gets the fun started from page one with a myriad of clever details."
—Publisher's Weekly

BOOKS BY LESLIE LANGTRY

Merry Wrath Mysteries
Merit Badge Murder
Mint Cookie Murder
Scout Camp Mystery
(short story in the "Killer Beach Reads" collection)

Greatest Hits Mysteries:
'Scuse Me While I Kill This Guy
Guns Will Keep Us Together
Stand By Your Hitman
I Shot You Babe
Paradise By The Rifle Sights
Snuff The Magic Dragon
My Heroes Have Always Been Hitmen
Four Killing Birds (holiday short story)
Have Yourself a Deadly little Chrsitmas

Other Works:
Sex, Lies, & Family Vacations

Hanging Tree Tales YA horror novels:
Hell House
Tyler's Fate
Witch Hill
The Teacher

MINT COOKIE MURDER

a Merry Wrath mystery

Leslie Langtry

This book is dedicated to the girls of my Girl Scout troop. For 10 years you put up with me, and you gave me memories I will never, ever, ever forget (as well as LOTS of material for these books)! I love you all!

CHAPTER ONE

——

As a former CIA operative, I've heard a lot of statements that have chilled me as though I had a foot-long icicle down my throat while sitting naked and wet on an ice floe. (By the way—don't go to Greenland. Ever.) Things like, *Open up! It's the police, and we have a flamethrower!* and *Tell me the code or I'll have to use this pair of pliers on your eyelids.* All terrifying under normal circumstances, but throw in the Iranian secret police or a Venezuelan death squad dressed as circus clowns, and they have a smidge more gravitas.

But nothing...*nothing* compares to what I was just told.

"What do you mean we have to sell cookies?" I asked Kelly with a slight tremble in my voice. "To people? On *purpose*?"

My best friend and co-leader rolled her eyes. "Girl Scout Cookies. Our troop has to sell them."

"Why on Earth would we want to do that?" I asked, backing up against the kitchen wall. I was starting to regret never having put in hidden panels with weapons around the house. But then Kelly would just laugh at me if I pulled a garrote on her.

"Because it's a fundraiser for us and for the Council." She pointed to the stack of order forms and the colorful brochure showing the prizes the girls get for selling so many boxes. I started flipping through the flier. Tiny pewter owls? Why does a little girl need one tiny pewter owl? Unless the purpose is to melt it down into one tiny, pewter bullet—then it sorta makes sense. And what's with all the sticker books? Diabolical! I can only see a child's access to 101 stickers turning into a nightmare of epic proportions. Oh wait! Dora the Explorer stickers! I looked up at my Dora bedsheet curtains and cringed. I really need to buy drapes.

"How do we sell cookies?" I asked. "Set up a store somewhere?" I had no idea how something like this worked. It kinda sounded like a scam, actually. Selling certain cookies only one time a year. Give them a taste, and then demand turns into desperation. Hmmm...also diabolical. I knew international villains who could learn something from the Girl Scouts.

"We go door-to-door," Kelly sighed. "Take the forms to work. Call our friends and beg or blackmail them."

Definitely a scam. I shook my head. "I don't have any friends besides you, Rex, and Riley." I wondered if I had enough blackmail material to get Riley to take the form to Langley to sell among the other spooks. I mean, I had some good stuff (like photos from the time he overused self-tanner for a job on the Riviera and looked like an Oompa Loompa), but did I have enough?

"Wait!" I said as I studied the form. "People have to give their names, addresses, and phone numbers?" No one in the CIA would do that. We can't even tell spouses and children what we do for a living.

"You'll have to do it." I shoved the whole mess toward my best friend and troop co-leader. "I'll do the behind the scenes work. Like the incentives and inventory, fear and intimidation, blackmail sales, wet work, and stuff."

Kelly rolled her eyes. I got the distinct impression she wasn't taking me seriously. "No wet work—no spy stuff! We're just selling cookies!"

I winked at her. "Right." I placed my index finger on my lips and looked around. "Just selling cookies." I winked again for emphasis.

Kelly rolled her eyes and sighed the sigh of 100 martyrs. "Look, we have to do it. I know you don't want to. But it's non-negotiable. If you want to do all the things you've planned with this troop and you don't want to pay for it yourself, we have to do this fundraiser."

She put her hands on her hips, a sign I knew meant that this conversation was over, and I had lost. And she was right. Even if she wasn't. Kelly was right. She always won.

"I'm not planning anything expensive..." I moped.

My best friend's right eyebrow bent upwards. "Oh really? What about the winter survival skills campout?"

I shrugged. "That's a totally legit idea."

"In Newfoundland?" Kelly asked. "And your equipment list is ridiculous." She numbered the items off. "Snow shoes and cross-country skis for each girl...sleeping bags with a 50-degrees-below-zero rating...white sniper camouflage suits..."

"Hey!" I protested. "Those are important!"

Kelly ignored me. "And I'm not even going to mention flying in some Israeli Mossad agent you know to teach a weekend-long class on self-defense to second-grade girls."

I lifted my chin and sniffed. "It's called Krav Maga—and he's the world's foremost expert. How do you expect these girls to survive a kidnapping attempt?"

Kelly narrowed her eyes. *Uh-oh. Why did I have to bring that up?*

"Well, I guess they could've used that a few months ago when you dragged them into a gunfight with the CIA and local SWAT team."

I slumped. She was right. Totally my fault there. I still felt bad for that one. It didn't matter that the girls thought it had been the best day of their lives.

Kelly's voice softened. "Look, all I'm saying is that these things cost money. And we can raise some of that by doing what Girl Scouts have been doing for a century—selling cookies."

"Fine," I grumbled. "But you have to be in charge."

"Okay. But I'm not doing *everything*," Kelly agreed. "I'll talk about it at the troop meeting."

A couple of months ago, my life had been pretty uneventful. I was your typical, disavowed CIA agent who moved back to Who's There, Iowa in disguise and under an assumed name. Kelly was the only person I grew up with who knew who I really was. That isn't as unusual as it may sound. No one really knew who I was when I lived here as a kid. I didn't have many friends and was kind of a wallflower—if wallflower means I was invisible (which, by the way, would've been an awesome superpower to have as a secret agent). My dad, a United States senator, didn't even start running for office until I'd gone off to college. And by then, he'd moved to Des Moines—the big city.

As for relatives—we only had my mom's family, and they all lived in Maryland. Never set foot in Iowa. My dad was an only child and my grandparents, long gone. I had a tiny connection to this community, which was a benefit as far as I was concerned.

Anywhoo...I lived here completely under the radar and helped Kelly with her Girl Scout troop. That is, until someone started knocking off major international terrorists in my backyard and the CIA sent my former hottie handler, Riley Andrews, to babysit me.

"How's the dating thing going with Rex?" Kelly asked with a wink.

I shrugged. "Good, I guess." Rex was the gorgeous police detective who lived across the street.

"We hang out at his house every Saturday night with a rented movie and carryout," I said cautiously. My previous line of work as a secret agent still kicked in from time to time, and I didn't want to jinx it by telling Kelly too much.

Not that there was much to tell. We actually just spent Saturdays at his house, watching movies and eating. Rex said it was because he was out around town all the time with work and liked relaxing at home and getting to know me. But for this girl, whose dates have included dodging bullets at a Polish fusion restaurant in Tel Aviv and dancing the rhumba with diplomats at a NATO gala, things were getting a little dull.

"Sounds cozy..." Kelly smiled.

"You got that right," I answered. I'd virtually memorized everything in Rex's living room, from the candlesticks that could be used as weapons to how long it would take us to get out through the side windows if attacked by North Korean spies or spider monkeys armed with blow darts (which, it might surprise you to know, can actually be the same thing).

Kelly frowned and studied me. "Not going well?"

I shrugged again. "We have fun. He's great to hang out with. We fool around a little." Rex was a great kisser. We hadn't taken it much further than making out though. I wasn't going to tell her I was getting worried. Let her think everything's fine.

"I just thought dating a detective would be a little more exciting." You know, I really have no idea what I'm going to say sometimes.

My best friend's right eyebrow arched sharply. "Exciting? I thought you didn't want that."

I waited for her to once again remind me of the mess that happened a few months ago, but she didn't say anything.

"Well, what about Riley?" Kelly said with a wicked grin.

I glared at her, but she just gave me that look that said *answer-the-question-cuz-I'm-not-going-to-drop-it-til-you-do.* I hated that look.

"Riley is...well, that's complicated," I finally answered. A few months ago, it seemed like my former handler was interested in me. But I hadn't heard from him in over four weeks. He'd said something about a lead on Midori Ito—a Yakuza boss who'd rudely showed up murdered in my kitchen a short while ago. We'd never solved that murder, and Riley was on the case. Part of me got that he was a working CIA operative, often sent out of country on assignments for long periods of time. But the other part of me was a little more needy than that.

"I think he's been out of town on assignment," I said in hopes of ending this line of questioning. "Which is fine because I'm seeing Rex." And that was true. I didn't really want a love triangle, did I?

Kelly nodded. "Fine. I've got to go anyway." She put on her coat and headed for the door. "Read over the stuff for the meeting. We've got to go over this with the girls." And then she left.

I carried the Girl Scout materials, a bottle of wine, and a plate full of Pizza Rolls with a healthy dollop of three-cheese ranch dressing out to the living room and put them down on my new coffee table.

That's right. I'd finally bought furniture! Okay, well, I'd bought a coffee table. Kelly had taken me to IKEA a few weeks ago. Her argument was that since I now had a boyfriend of sorts, I should have furniture that a grown-up would have. We spent hours in showroom after showroom before I finally freaked out and bought one tiny table for my living room and threatened her with a stapler if we didn't leave immediately. That was it.

Have you ever been in one of those places? I felt like I was being assaulted by furniture and designers. How the hell does someone survive a place like that? I suppose if you were wealthy, you could just pick out whole rooms and have them delivered. But I couldn't do that. Oh sure, I had money, but I had no idea if those whole rooms would work in my house. Wouldn't I have to measure or something? And if it all didn't fit, how on Earth would I decide what goes and what doesn't?

Kelly was slightly less than happy with me as we drove three hours home with one box containing the pieces and parts for a coffee table. She didn't even offer to help me put it together. I didn't want to ask Rex because I wanted to surprise him with my new "grown-up" status as a responsible furniture owner.

It took me five days to put the damn thing together. I'm not kidding. And when I got it done, it looked less like a table and more like something Picasso had drawn after ingesting LSD and chasing it with absinthe. Still, it stood and wobbled a only little. Well, it wobbled only a little once I put a 9mm magazine under one of the legs.

I haven't unveiled it to Rex yet. I'm waiting to do a big *ta-da* when I get a lamp or something. I want to really blow his mind.

The doorbell rang, and I paused with a mouthful of Pizza Rolls. Who could that be? Kelly must've forgotten something. I wiped my mouth on my sleeve, because I'd forgotten napkins again, and made my way toward the door.

I couldn't see anything out of my security peephole in the door. That's weird. Was it a little kid? I took a chance and opened the door.

"Please..." A man lay bleeding on my porch. He reached toward me with bloody fingers. "Help..." His eyes grew wide when he saw my face, just before the light went out of them and he collapsed, lifeless.

I stepped over him and looked around the neighborhood. There was no one there. A long, bloody trail led from a beat-up, orange hatchback in my driveway. This guy hadn't been delivered here by someone else. He drove here. To my house.

I pulled my cell phone out, dialed, and watched until the lights came on in the house directly across the street.

"Hey, Merry!" Rex answered. His deep, sexy voice usually took my breath away, but not this time. Okay...so maybe it did...a little.

"Rex," I said without any pleasantries. "Do you remember hearing about Lenny Smith?"

"The spy who sold all those tech secrets from Silicon Valley to the Chinese? Yeah." His voice was a little more guarded now, which was depressing.

"You might want to come over," I said with a sigh. "He's dead on my front porch."

CHAPTER TWO

———

Rex arrived in under a minute—which I guess makes sense since he lives so close. He'd been shaving and was wiping off the last of the shaving cream as he crossed the street. Why was he doing that? It was seven o'clock at night. Did he have plans? I didn't remember him asking me over...

The local police arrived one minute after that. They swarmed my porch, under Rex's direction, while I stood in the doorway watching. My cell rang.

"Wrath." Riley's measured tones told me he wasn't happy. "What the hell?"

"How did you find out so fast?" I asked, looking around my doorframe. Had he installed cameras or something? Hey! I was mad at him! No calls for weeks, but the minute there's a dead body...

"Kelly called," Riley answered. I looked out and sure enough, Kelly was standing in my front yard, hands on her hips. Damn. That woman should've been in the CIA instead of me.

"Yeah, well the police are handling it," I said a little snippily.

Rex stepped up to me. "I've got to go, Riley," I said as I hung up on him. That felt good.

"Why don't you go sit down by your cat?" Rex said.

I frowned. "I don't have a cat."

He pointed at the couch. "Well, there's one right now, eating your...Pizza Rolls? You're eating Pizza Rolls?"

I turned to see a very, very large black and white cat lapping up the ranch dressing on my plate.

"When did you get a cat? I was just here, and you didn't say anything about a cat!" Kelly yelled from my kitchen. She must've decided to circumvent the porch by coming in the back door. She came around the corner and stopped, jaw open, when she spotted the animal. Apparently, that was more shocking than having a dead man on my porch.

I ran over to the table and tried to shoo the animal away. He looked up at me and sat down on his haunches. Then, ignoring me, he proceeded to clean his paws.

"Scat! Go away!" I even hissed at him. The cat acted like I wasn't even there.

"I like him," Kelly said.

"He must've wandered in somehow," I said, still waving my arms as if that was working—which it wasn't. "Maybe he was with Lenny?" I turned to Kelly, "You ever see him before? In the neighborhood?"

Kelly shook her head. She walked over to the couch and sat down beside the feline intruder, who now seemed to notice her. Kelly scratched between his ears, and he responded by purring louder than a rumbling garbage truck and closing one eye—keeping one yellow eye narrowed at me. Smart cat—never taking his eye off his adversary.

"Well he can't stay here," I said.

Rex joined me. He glanced at the cat, then the table, and then me. "Did you get a table?"

He noticed!

"I did! Kelly took me shopping." Maybe I shouldn't have said that. Maybe a grown-up goes shopping for furniture on her own.

Detective Hottie shook his head. "I can come over later and fix it for you."

Fix it for me?

He continued before I could respond, "I've already gotten your statement so you don't have to go downtown. We'll take the body to the coroner now. We've documented everything, so you can clean up if you like."

I nodded. "Okay. Can you tell me how he died?" I had some suspicions. From the way he fell, the bloody smears on the sidewalk, and the holes in the back of his coat, I knew he'd been shot. Small caliber, definitely. That's why he didn't die immediately. But I wasn't going to say anything because I'd read in my online research that men don't like women upstaging them in their own profession. Which was totally stupid, but I was trying to be a supportive girlfriend.

"Looks like he's been shot." Rex said with a wink. "But I'm sure you knew that already." He squeezed my arm affectionately and headed for the doorway. He smelled good. Too good. And I remembered that he'd been shaving when I called him.

"You smell good," I ventured. "Why were you shaving at seven o'clock at night?"

"Oh yeah." He grinned. "I was getting ready to go out."

"Did we have plans?" *Oh crap.* Had I forgotten? I should probably buy a calendar too.

"No," he said simply. "An old friend is in town, and I was going to meet her for a couple of drinks. I'll have to reschedule now."

Her? Did he say *her*?

"I've got to get to the office," Rex said as he glanced at his watch. "I'll call you later, okay?" He kissed me on the cheek and headed out the door. I heard a loud, deep *meooooooooooooow* behind me. It sounded like a goat being castrated. And yes, I once had to help castrate goats as part of my cover. That's right. I can castrate a goat, but I can't put a coffee table together. Sad, right?

"Hey, wait!" I called after him. "Aren't you going to take the cat?"

"No," Rex called from the porch. "We don't know that it's the victim's. But keep it around just in case I need to interview him." He was gone before I could respond to that.

"You said you wanted a cat," Kelly said from the couch. I turned and glared at her.

"I was just *thinking* about getting a cat. I didn't mean it."

The beast opened his other eye and gave me his full attention. It was unnerving.

"He's got a Hitler mustache!" I pointed at the perfect, black rectangle below his nose and a dark patch on his head that looked like hair. "I can't keep a Nazi cat! I'm a Girl Scout leader. I need to have standards."

Kelly shook her head and started scratching the cat's chin. He responded by purring again. "He does! How cute! Who's a cute wittle kitty-cat? You are!" Her voice sounded like a creepy little kid's. "He looks kind of like Charlie Chaplin with that hair too."

I looked at the black spot on his head. "No. Chaplin's hair was parted down the middle. This cat's is parted on the side. Just like Hitler."

Kelly hoisted the enormous cat onto her lap and smiled. "It doesn't matter—he's adorable. Not his fault the way his markings are."

"Okay—so *you* take Adolf," I said. "He likes you."

My best friend gave me an exasperated look. "My husband's allergic to cats. You know that." She stood up and put on her coat—a move the cat clearly protested by yowling loudly. "And don't call him Adolf. He doesn't like it. Come on. Let's go to the pet store."

I stared at her. "You can't be serious."

But she was. Ten minutes later we were standing in the feline aisle of the local pet store. I went along because I had no choice. What was I going to do? Throw the animal out? Not in front of Kelly. The truth was, I'd never had a pet before (well, except for a brief stint with a llama named Rooster when I was stationed in the Andes—but that's better left unmentioned). Both parents were allergic to anything with fur, and I wasn't interested in the kind that was hairless. Turtles, snakes, and lizards didn't scare me, but they didn't turn me into a mushy mess who wanted an animal to cuddle.

"Rex is going to have drinks with a woman," I said as I played with a feathery cat toy.

"I heard him say that," Kelly grunted, heaving a huge box of cat litter into the cart. It fell with a thunk to the bottom. Well, if it didn't work out with the cat, I could always tie it to the cat litter box and throw it into the river.

"You don't think that's bad?" I asked, tossing the feather toy into the cart. "It doesn't sound good to me."

Kelly rolled her eyes. "He told you about it, didn't he? He's not hiding anything."

"Oh—he's definitely hiding something," I said. "He only mentioned it because I caught him."

"You are so suspicious. Caught him doing what, exactly?" Kelly asked. "Investigating the dead guy on your porch?"

"That is not my fault. Besides, it's my job to be suspicious. And by the way—why in hell did you call Riley? And since when are you calling Riley?"

She shrugged. "Since he asked me to keep an eye on you. He can help."

"Riley hasn't shown any interest in me lately—until something happened that might embarrass the agency. I don't want his help." I ignored the little twinge of sadness in my gut. Yes, it bothered me that Riley hadn't stuck around. But I was getting over that. Now he'd come barging back into my life, batting those blue eyes at me and kissing me when I least expected it, and I'd end up all confused again.

We pulled up into the driveway with bags of stuff, got out of Kelly's car, and followed Dead Lenny's bloody stain up the sidewalk to the front door.

"You should probably clean that up," Kelly said.

"I want to look at it a little more closely," I responded as we went inside and dropped everything on the kitchen counter.

"Well get out there and do it before the neighborhood starts a petition to run you out," Kelly said as she began to set up the litter box. It had a hood with a hole in the front of it. Like a little kitty hut, but for a giant cat with possible fascist dictator tendencies. I left Kelly to it and went outside.

The police had towed the orange car away to check for evidence. Drops of blood began where the driver's side would've been. About halfway to the front door, he must've collapsed to the ground, because that's where the smearing started. I knew he'd been shot, and from the blood loss he probably had trouble walking. So why come here? Why me? It didn't make any sense.

Kelly appeared with a bucket of bleach and a broom. She watched as I scrubbed the stains out. They didn't disappear completely. But at least it no longer looked like I was butchering people in my driveway. I couldn't imagine the neighbors liked that much. Hmmm...this might negatively impact my Girl Scout Cookie sales.

We went back inside to find the cat sniffing around the litter box. He looked up at us for a moment, and deciding we weren't interesting, wandered inside the box. Only his tail stuck out through the hood. How did he fit his enormous bulk in there?

"You'll have to take him to a vet and get him looked over," Kelly said as she gathered up her things.

"I thought I'd wait, and maybe he'd just, you know, go home." The cat stuck his head out of the box and glared. I think he heard me. I knew nothing about cats. Were they into revenge? I'd have to do some research.

"Don't wait. He could be sick or something," she said. "Call Dr. Rye. I've heard he's excellent."

"Well, he's certainly not anorexic," I mumbled. This cat resembled a basketball that sprouted fur. He wasn't *in* shape. He was *a* shape...round.

"I'll call the local shelter and see if anyone reported him missing. And the vet can scan him for a chip."

"A chip? Like a tracking device? That's pretty cool. Where do they put it? Does it explode if the cat does something unsavory?" The idea of an embedded, exploding tracking device was kind of fun.

Kelly ignored me. "There's no collar, so maybe he did show up with the dead guy. In which case—the cat is probably yours now. You should think of a name."

"How about Kitler?" I suggested.

"Enough with the Nazi references. You'll hurt his feelings." And with that, she walked out the door.

"I'm not going to name a cat that'll be leaving soon," I grumbled as I grabbed my laptop and headed for the couch. The animal had eaten all my pizza rolls and licked up every drop of ranch dressing. Great. My guess was he'd probably be in that litter box for a while. I had some time to look up the bastard who'd inconsiderately died on my front stoop.

Lenny Smith had been busted under the CIA's watch with two other agents. I'd had nothing to do with his capture. He'd been an IT geek who worked at different times for all the big companies in Silicon Valley. No one seemed to notice how much he job-hopped. I guess that was normal in the field. It wasn't until Cy Stern, a colleague of mine who specialized in Asian languages, started noticing a lot of chatter by the Chinese about a mole in the IT industry.

Cy was a great agent. He followed Smith all over Beijing and produced enough intel for the FBI to stage a little welcome home party for Lenny when he flew back to San Francisco. Unfortunately, Cy didn't get the credit because, you know, undercover crap and all. But trust me, he did all the heavy lifting.

When I said Lenny was a geek, I meant it. A little, mousy guy with a beer belly and receding hairline, he wore Google glasses all the time and had a fashion sense lost somewhere in the late '80s. In spite of this, he managed the largest tech heist ever across five of the big companies.

The last I'd heard, he was someone's "girlfriend" in prison. So how was he out and dead here in Iowa? The networks hadn't picked up the story yet. I was pretty sure Rex was keeping this in lockdown. He probably didn't tell anyone who he was.

I should call him.

"Merry?" Rex asked, picking up on the first ring.

"Oh, hey," I tried to sound sheepish. "Sorry for the extra work tonight. Can you talk?"

"Not really." There was a smile in his voice. "I rescheduled meeting my friend. This is going to take a while. Hold on a sec."

Oh, no. I ruined his meeting with "her." So sad.

"Sorry. I didn't want the guys to hear. I'm not releasing the name of the victim yet. Thought I'd give you a head start before the media started pestering you."

Awww! What a thoughtful guy! "Thanks. Any chance you can avoid saying where the body was found?"

"For a little while, at least," Rex responded. "I've called the Feds. They're sending their local guys over."

"There are local guys?" I asked. I didn't think small-town Iowa had any agents, but I didn't mix well with the Feds. Most CIA employees don't.

"Yeah. There's an office in Des Moines," he said. "They don't want the word out before they understand what exactly happened."

"What do you mean?"

"I mean that until this happened, no one at the prison even knew Lenny was gone. They thought he was in his cell right up until the moment I called them, and I told him he wasn't there."

CHAPTER THREE

———

The doorbell rang. I thanked my adorable boyfriend, and he promised to stop by once he got off work to check in.

"Riley," I said, my face falling as I answered the door. My former handler flashed his blue-eyed golden boy smile at me and stepped inside. He was wearing a white, button-down shirt with pressed khakis. And he was carrying a suitcase.

"Hello, Wrath." Riley said as he shut the door behind him and set down the suitcase. "Guess what? I'm moving in."

"What?" I stepped backward, shaking my head. "No. You aren't. You can go to a hotel. You can't stay here." A dead traitor shows up on my doorstep, and he thinks that's an invitation to play house?

"You've got an extra bedroom," he said as he made his way down the hall. "The agency wants me to monitor you closely."

"I don't work for the agency anymore. I don't know why I have to keep telling you that," I snarled.

He shook his head. "Doesn't matter. You're still a person of interest. We still haven't explained Midori, and now you have dead traitors showing up at your house."

Midori Ito, head of the Yakuza, had made an appearance as a dead woman in my kitchen a few months ago. We thought she'd been tied to another case at the time, but she wasn't. She'd been here for reasons we didn't yet understand. Riley and I ditched the body in Chicago, and she hadn't been found, but this was somehow considered my fault.

"This is a bad idea, Riley," I said. "I've started sleepwalking with knives—you could end up stabbed in your sleep 40 or 50 times," I lied.

"Okay, Lizzie Borden. I'll keep my door locked." He set his suitcase down on the bed and headed for the kitchen with me trailing behind him. He stopped dead in his tracks at the breakfast bar, and I plowed into him.

"Whoa," he said. I followed his eyes to see the cat sitting in the middle of the breakfast bar, narrowing his eyes at Riley.

"That's my new attack cat. I don't think he likes you. You should go," I said quickly.

As if sensing my disapproval of the situation, the animal hissed. Maybe he wasn't so bad after all.

Riley reached out, and the cat leaned into him, eyes closed and purring like a semi with a bad muffler. Now that was a real traitor.

"I like cats," Riley said as the fat beast dropped and exposed his belly. Stupid cat! "What's his name? He kind of looks like Hitler."

"He showed up when Lenny did. I've never seen him before, but Rex wants me to keep an eye on him."

Riley frowned and ran his hands over the animal, who purred even louder. "Did you search him?"

I stared at him. "Search who? The cat? Are you serious?" I was more pissed at myself than him. I'd seen animals used as everything from messengers to drug mules. Why hadn't I thought of that?

Riley gave me a glance that intimated that maybe I was an idiot. I walked over to the "everything" drawer and pulled out a pair of latex gloves.

"Okay," I said, tossing them to him. "Show me how it's done."

"I am not doing a cavity search on a cat." Riley ignored the gloves. "Just check the litter box in a couple of days."

There was no way I was doing that. No way. Not a chance.

I changed the subject. "You can't move in here, Riley. This is my house. And I don't work for you. You have no rights here."

Riley sat down at the breakfast bar. The cat came closer to him, purring so loudly I could barely hear. Great.

"Tell me what happened with Lenny," he said.

I sighed and sat down next to him. It took me about five minutes to tell him everything I knew...which wasn't a lot. The cat started rubbing all over Riley like the tanned blond with wavy hair was covered in tuna. Every now and then, the beast would stop and glare at me.

"He doesn't like you," Riley said with something I interpreted as satisfaction.

"The feeling's mutual," I said, glaring back as the cat ignored me.

"Why? You told me you wanted to get a cat."

Yes. I had told him that. "I wanted to get a nice cat. Maybe start with a kitten. I didn't want to inherit a possible double-crossing beast like this."

Riley smiled at the animal. "It couldn't have been Lenny's. The supermax, ADX Florence in Colorado, didn't even know he was out. There wasn't enough time for him to adopt a cat."

"Well, he made it from California to here in an orange hatchback," I said. "He could've picked up a cat along the way."

"That's true." Riley nodded. "But according to prison officials, Lenny was at roll call this morning."

"Maybe he could time travel. Maybe the cat's some sort of evil wizard," I suggested. I'd been reading a lot of science fiction lately and even binge-watched *Battlestar Galactica* in a marathon session that had me glued to the couch for a week.

"Well, it couldn't have been Lenny at the prison. Not if he was here. They obviously made a mistake. Probably covering it up." He scratched the cat behind the ears. "Something's going on," Riley mused. "I think we need to get this kitty scanned."

"That's what Kelly said."

He nodded. "Dr. Rye is who she recommended." Riley started dialing his cell before I could ask whether Kelly was spying for him or if my kitchen was bugged. Either way, I was going to make sure he bought a couple dozen cases of Girl Scout Cookies.

"I don't like it, Ms. Wrath," Dr. Rye said for the fourth time as he felt up my cat on the exam table. The 50-something veterinarian talked like a game show host with a loud, dramatic flourish at the end that for some reason made me hold my breath. And every now and then he would walk over to the wall, turn his back toward us, and shake his head. It was weird. But then, this was my first veterinarian. Maybe they're all like this.

"Nope. I don't like it," he repeated gravely as if asking a giant board if there was a letter *M* and waiting for Vanna to make her move.

I glared at Riley before turning to the vet. "You keep saying that. What do you mean exactly?"

Dr. Rye looked over his glasses at me, arching his right, very scary bushy eyebrow. Maybe he kept gerbils in there. "He's obese. That's bad."

"That's not why we brought..." I really couldn't name him Hitler. "...Philby here." I heard Riley snort behind me. I ignored it. "Can you scan him for a chip?"

The vet nodded like a deranged bobblehead for a minute solid before leaving the room. He returned a couple of minutes later with a green, hand-held device and held it over the cat's neck.

"There is something there." The doc frowned and began to feel around Philby the Fat Cat's neck. The beast did nothing. He'd behaved like an angel the whole time we'd been here. What a con artist.

"I'm not getting a reading. Must just be an anomaly. If it was an identification chip, we'd have the info. He's got some sort of fatty buildup in his neck. That must be it."

Riley stepped forward. "Thanks Dr. Rye." He lifted Philby as if the animal had always been his. The cat purred and would've probably snuggled up if he could've bent his midsection. However, it's impossible to fold a basketball in half, so Riley just had to settle for the idea that the cat liked him.

"I want you to schedule a full checkup for Philby," Dr. Rye said before walking out the door and leaving us standing in the room.

As I paid the bill, the nurse handed me a card for an appointment. I slid it into my back pocket and joined Riley and the cat in Riley's rented SUV.

"Philby?" Riley asked as he started the car. "You named him after a Communist double agent who betrayed Great Britain? Why?"

"Hey, it's better than Hitler," I grumbled. "Besides," I said as I gave the cat a look, "I don't really know whose side he's on now, do I?"

Philby was sitting on the floor between the two seats. He looked up at me and gave me a loud *meeeoooooow*, then began to lick his front paw, which was all he could really reach.

We pulled into the garage, and the three of us made our way back into the house. Riley set the beast down, and Philby trotted over to his litter box and went in. I thought about what Riley had said earlier about me checking his crap for clues. The hell I would.

It was getting late. I supposed I should be thinking about dinner, but I was wondering how to do that with a guest in the house. I didn't really have anything besides junk food. And we still hadn't sorted out the fact that Riley mistakenly thought he was moving in.

"Are you selling Girl Scout Cookies?" Riley's voice brought me back to reality.

Damn. I'd forgotten. "Yes, and I'm putting you down for a dozen cases. Go ahead and pick the kind you want because that's what you're buying."

He frowned as he looked at the forms. "Oh my God! Look at these ingredients! You can't expect me to eat these! Don't they make any that are all natural?"

I shook my head. "Nope. And if you don't pick a flavor, I'll do it for you."

"What the hell am I going to do with a dozen cases of chemicals?" Riley asked.

"I have a few ideas..." I mumbled.

Riley ignored me and started going through my cupboards, ending with the refrigerator. He pulled out his cell phone and dialed.

"You have no food here," he said to me as he waited.

"I have plenty of food here," I protested.

He shook his head. "No, you have crap here. Chemical particles loosely held together by what used to be food. Tomorrow, we're going shopping. I can't live like this."

"You aren't supposed to." I put my hands on my hips in an attempt to look threatening. "This is my house. You do not live here," I said, emphasizing each word independently so he'd know.

Riley shook his head and turned away from me. In perfect Mandarin Chinese, he ordered a complete takeout dinner, sans the MSG. When he hung up, he smirked.

"It'll be here in 20 minutes. Just enough time for me to unpack. I ordered three dinners."

"Three?" I asked.

He nodded. "Rex is walking over right now." And with that, he disappeared down the hallway. The bastard.

I threw my hands in the air and stomped very maturely over to the door. I opened it as Rex was lifting his hand to knock. He kissed me then walked right in. This was getting out of hand. It was bad enough that Kelly came and went as she pleased, but to have these two men doing it? I was definitely going to have to wire the doorknob to shock, based on these two's biometrics. They'd learn soon enough.

The Chinese was delivered, and the three of us settled in the kitchen, Riley and Rex on the stools at the breakfast bar, me standing on the other side. I should probably get a table with chairs.

Rex filled Riley in on how he found Lenny on my doorstep after he'd called.

"He'd escaped from the supermax in Colorado," Rex said as he pushed away his plate. "They aren't sure how. Coroner says he was shot somewhere else, drove here, and died of blood loss from three gunshot wounds. All through the back."

"Have you made a statement to the press?" I asked. I was not looking forward to another glut of media on my front yard like I'd had a few months ago.

"Tomorrow," Rex said. "We're not going to say where he was found, as a matter of national interest. That should keep the reporters away from you for a while."

I started putting the leftover food in the fridge. "I just don't understand why he came here. I had nothing to do with Lenny. Riley had another agent on that case."

Riley nodded. "It doesn't make sense. How would a prisoner in lockdown find you, anyway? We've managed to keep your cover intact even with the last situation. No one but the guys at the top in the agency know where you are. Or *who* you are."

"Maybe there's a leak?" Rex mused. "The commissioner wants this wrapped up on our end. He doesn't want to tap into another event with Feds."

I turned to Riley. "You should go to Colorado and check his visitor logs, phone calls, stuff like that." That would get him out of my house.

"There's no leak at the top," Riley said. "I think there's still some connection to the problems we had here a few months ago. Someone who's after you is still alive."

"Oh, come on!" I protested. "That's got to be over!"

Riley gave me a look that said, *Oh yeah? What about Midori?*

I gave him a look that said, *Shut up!*

Rex looked from me to Riley. "Well, whatever's going on, I'd like you to come by the station and take this off our hands."

"Wait…" I said as I realized something. "Did you know Riley was coming here?"

Rex nodded. "He called me. That's why I'm here for dinner."

Did everyone know what was going on except for me? Kelly and Riley were talking…Rex and Riley were talking…for all I knew, Philby was talking to someone who still wanted me dead, or worse.

"Hey!" Rex said, reaching for the Girl Scout forms. "Are you selling cookies?"

I glared at my boyfriend. "Yes. And you're buying two cases." That showed him.

CHAPTER FOUR

———

After Rex left and Riley went to bed, I thought about the last 24 hours.

A couple of months ago my life was fairly normal—well, as normal as it could be for an outed CIA agent living under a new identity in the middle of Iowa. Born as Fionnaghuala Merrygold Wrath Czrygy, I'm now Merry Wrath. My life as a spy with the CIA came to an end when a White House official outed me due to my father's lack of support on Capitol Hill. I was "retired" by the agency with a nice settlement, and I moved back to my hometown of Who's There—a small city in Iowa—to help my best friend run a Girl Scout troop. And it worked out nicely...for a year.

Then, dead terrorists started showing up on my doorstep. Three of them, to be exact. I was mobbed by the media, squeezed by the local police—which led me to meeting my boyfriend, Detective Rex Ferguson—and almost, sorta seduced by my former agency handler, Riley Andrews.

The whole mess was wrapped up after an embarrassing shootout that unfortunately involved my second-grade Girl Scout troop, but everything ended okay—I guess. Things have been somewhat quiet since then. Until today.

Now the whole mess was starting to come back. That sucked.

I made sure to kiss Rex good-bye in front of Riley, who looked at me strangely before he went to bed. I didn't see him the next morning, as he left a note on the breakfast counter that said he was off to the police station. Good. Let the agency deal with this. It wasn't my problem. Well, except for the fact the guy died on my stoop. I met Kelly at the school for our Girl Scout meeting.

"*Cookies*!" The girls yelled in unison as we passed out the samples the Council had given us. Kelly handed out juice boxes and cookie forms and started talking about how we would handle the sales.

"Mrs. Wrath?" Kaitlin asked. She was one of the four Kaitlins. I wasn't sure which. All four of them had brown hair and blue eyes, and their last names inexplicably all began with the letter *G.*

And all of them called me "Mrs.," no matter how hard I tried to correct them. I was at the point of considering electric shock negative reinforcement, but Kelly sort of frowned on that idea. I'd have to find something that wouldn't get me in trouble.

"Yes?" I asked.

"Do we get to eat all the cookies we sell?" Kaitlin the Second finished the question for Kaitlin. The other girls nodded as if they, too, were thinking the exact same thing.

"Only if you buy them. You can only eat the cookies you buy. You can't eat the cookies other people buy from you."

"Why?" Kaitlin Three asked.

"Because they aren't yours," I answered. The fourth Kaitlin was thankfully silent.

"Do we get to keep the money?" Hannah asked. "I want to buy a puppy."

I could see the logic in that. "No. The money goes to our troop so we can do fun things."

"Like shoot guns in school again?" Emily's eyes sparkled, and the whole group of girls burst into a loud cheer.

"No," I said. "And don't mention that to your parents. Please."

Kelly spoke up. "Now ladies, when you sell, make sure you always have a parent with you. I don't want you going door-to-door alone."

"Right!" Anna shouted. "We need backup. Always bring backup."

"Shouldn't we pack heat?" Ava asked. "Would you recommend a 9 millimeter or a .38?"

Personally, I'd go with a .45 Glock (although I was rather partial to the Colt Gold Cup), but Ava was new to this, so I cut her some slack. Kelly interrupted and told the girls they weren't to bring weapons of any kind. Then she glared at me, which I thought was a little unfair.

"How about a sharpened screwdriver?" Betty asked.

"Or a shiv made out of wood?" Lauren suggested.

Apparently, recess chatter mirrored *Orange Is the New Black*. Kind of different than in my day when the biggest question was whether to play foursquare or jump rope.

"*No weapons of any kind!*" Kelly screamed. This got their attention. The girls stared at us in shock. Now *who was being a dick,* I thought.

Kelly decided this was a good time to hand out the coloring sheets that depicted happy, dancing cookies talking about sales. The girls immediately started adding handguns to the cookies' little stick arms. A couple of them had the cookies shooting each other and bleeding caramel on the floor.

"You suck," Kelly whispered to me under her breath.

"Yeah. I know," I admitted. Still, I was impressed with the level of violence that cookies could get up to. And the good thing about cookies killing each other was that the cleanup would be delicious.

I collected the coloring sheets and crayons. No point in letting the girls take the evidence home. Although, I was pretty sure the girls would color these pictures on their own when they left.

We played a couple of games that did not include weapons until the parents came by to pick up the girls. I handed each parent a permission form and cookie sales info telling them the sale started in two days.

"How do you think they'll do?" I asked as we started straightening up the tables and chairs.

"Sounds like they're going to form a brute squad who will intimidate their neighbors into buying using homemade shivs and zip guns."

I smirked. "Well, they could really only get away with that once. What's the real objective?"

Kelly shrugged. "We set a goal of 300 dollars in sales per girl. That should give us enough money to have some fun next year. But you and I should sell too. Just to make up for any slack."

"Oh sure," I said. "You can take the forms to the hospital and sell there. What am I supposed to do?"

"That's your problem," Kelly sniffed. That's when I realized she was pissed off at me.

"Okay, what's *your* problem?" I asked.

My best friend since elementary school looked at me for a moment. "It's nothing. I've just been working too hard."

Liar. I could smell a lie a mile away. And right now, Kelly was lying to me. Something was wrong. And she wasn't going to tell me what it was. How unlike her.

"Come on," I pressed. "I know when something's up with you."

She shook her head. "I'm fine. Just tired. That's all." She snapped her troop binder shut, and her body language told me this conversation was over. Great.

I made my way home wondering what could be bothering Kelly. Was she mad about my newest dead body? Was she worried about Rex and me? Was she jealous about Riley shacking up at my house? Wait, that couldn't be it. Could it?

Kelly and Riley were definitely friendly—but I always kind of saw that as a weird united front to annoy me. Riley hadn't contacted me in weeks. But he was in touch with Kelly. Was Kelly interested in Riley?

No. That couldn't be it. Kelly was happily married. Cheating on her husband was one of the unlikeliest things she could do. Right?

I shook my head to clear it. No way I was even thinking of considering such a thing. It had to be something else. But what? There was Philby. Maybe she didn't like how I treated him? Maybe she wanted him but was afraid to ask?

No. If Kelly wanted Philby—she'd just take him, knowing it would be with my blessing. That wasn't it. I thought about her actions during the scout meeting. Was she upset about something with the troop? I re-ran the meeting through my mind. It didn't seem plausible.

Oh my God. Maybe she's sick! Maybe she has cancer or something! Was that possible? I mean, she's a nurse. My heart started pounding. I couldn't imagine life without Kelly. Sure, for several years I hadn't been in touch because I was a spy, but I always knew she was there for me. Kelly was my only link to this town. The troop and Rex, well, they were new. Kelly was it. If something happened to her, I'd...I'd...

I shut my brain down. This kind of thinking was a bad idea. My best friend didn't have cancer. There was something else wrong. And unlikely as it was that she wasn't sharing it with me, I'd just have to wait until she was ready to confide. And if it didn't happen soon, I'd beat it out of her.

Philby greeted me when I walked in the door to the kitchen. He sat right in front of me so I couldn't get past him. His eyes were on mine. I sat down on the floor. It was time he and I had a little chat.

"What's up?" I said. I held out my hand.

Philby sniffed my fingers delicately. Once again, he made eye contact and let out a loud and long *meeooooooooooooow*, and then he farted like a punctured basketball and walked away. On the plus side, it was kind of nice to be welcomed home.

CHAPTER FIVE

Riley wasn't home. *Aaaarrrrgh!* Now I was thinking of this as Riley's home. I had to get that man out of here. But in the meantime I should probably get some groceries. If I waited for him to go with me, it would be like him bossing me around again. I couldn't have that…my plate was full, what with Kelly probably dying of a rare and bizarre form of cancer and a Hitler cat look-alike plotting against me.

I scooped up my keys and within minutes was at the grocery store. After snagging a cart, I started working through the aisles one by one. This was new. Usually I just made a beeline for the junk food areas. But I had some time, so I might as well go through every part of the store. It's always good to familiarize yourself with any place you frequent—find out where the exits and good places to hide are, figure out the best foods to use as weapons.

That's not as funny as it sounds. I once saw a guy killed with a carrot. It was a very long and pointy carrot, so you can guess the endless applications. I stopped at the produce area first. Miles of green, red, yellow, and orange spread before me like a weirdly shaming, healthy rainbow.

I suppose it wouldn't hurt to have a salad now and then. But how did you make a salad? I'd eaten in five-star restaurants all over the world, and I'd had a salad or two when my cover insisted upon it. But they were already prepared. No one ever handed me a recipe. I never thought I'd need one.

Well, how hard could it be? I knew what a salad looked like. First, I'd need something sort of leafy. No problem. There was a huge display of such stuff—featuring every shade of green imaginable. I read the labels: iceberg, spinach, baby butter, romaine, kale…the list went on and on. I grabbed the first one in front of me. It said *romaine*. That sounded like Romania, where I once had an assignment where I'd been undercover as a nun. I had to strangle a rival spy with my rosary beads. It's not as difficult as it sounds—the beads were strung with piano wire and the bad guy had a weak neck. I think I still have those beads somewhere.

Okay, so now I had the leafy part of the salad. I'd probably need something else. You can't just have lettuce and dressing—even I knew that. Some reds and purples caught my eye. Maybe it's a color thing, and I should get what will look nice on all that green. Let's see: turnips, eggplant, rutabagas…

Eggplant sounded horrible but was pretty, but I couldn't remember ever eating one in a salad. Instead I went with rutabagas because it had nice alliteration with the word *romaine*.

Excellent. I had the leaves and a vegetable. I started pacing up and down the aisle. I picked up a clump of carrots because they were extra pointy and who knows—I might need to defend myself in the kitchen without ready access to knives someday. I wondered how long these veggies were good for. Riley would probably know that. Hey! Riley eats romaine and rutabagas! Clearly, alliteration *was* the key to making a salad.

I got a little carried away, tossing rhubarb, raspberries, red peppers, and radishes in my cart. But I figured I now had the clue—you make a salad based on the first letter of the kind of leaf. Feeling triumphant, I made my way to the salad dressings.

This part was easy! Ranch! I already had that! But just in case plain ranch wasn't foodie enough for Riley, I took one of every flavor, three cheese, bleu cheese, zesty…every kind they had.

This was going better than I'd hoped. But just to be safe, I thought I'd better hit the health section. Then Riley would see what a great host I was—even if I was a host who didn't really want to be one.

I knew granola was healthy, so I threw that in the cart. There was something strange called "soymilk" so I picked that up too. Somewhere I'd seen something about flaxseed being good for you, so I grabbed a big bag. I had no idea what you did with this stuff, but Riley probably would pour it directly in his mouth. It didn't look like you could do much else. I also tossed in some tofu, greek yogurt, and quinoa.

Then I headed for my area and loaded up on Pizza Rolls, Bagel Bites, frozen pizza, ravioli that came in a can, and mac and cheese that came in a blue box. I added a case of pop and a small box of ginger tea and checked out.

I arrived home triumphantly, greeted by Philby as a conquering hero. Or at least, that's what I thought he was thinking. It was hard to tell what an obese cat who looked like an evil dictator was thinking. In all honesty, he just sat and watched me unload groceries. But I decided that he adored my food gathering abilities and left it at that.

I was putting the food away when I noticed a strange man standing in my backyard. He seemed to be looking on the ground for something. My yard was not easily accessible. It had a private alley just for me and was surrounded by high bushes.

I stuck a carrot in my back pocket, just in case, and very quietly made my way to the garage and out into the yard. I stood there, not 150 feet away, and watched as he continued to look around. Eventually, he saw me.

"Oh!" he cried out. "Sorry to trespass." He smiled and walked over to me, his hand held out. I shook it carefully. He was middle-aged and thin as a rail. Pewter gray hair stuck out all over his head as if it was trying to escape. He wore wrinkled khaki pants, dirty work boots, and a worn hoodie. And I'd never seen him before.

"I'm your neighbor." He threw a thumb over his left shoulder. "Thataway, a few blocks. Name's Bob."

"Hello, Bob," I said warily. "Looking for something?"

"Oh, that's Bob with three *B*s," he added, smiling again.

Right. Bob with three *B*s. Who did that? And was it Bbob or Bobb? It couldn't be Bbob. That looked too much like boob. I decided it must be Bobb.

"I don't think I've ever seen you around here before," I said.

"I work third shift over at the factory," he said, still smiling. Well, that would account for his clothes.

"Which one?" I asked. This town had five major factories. Not that it mattered. I didn't know anyone who worked there. But I just felt he was too vague.

"Greenplow," he said, as he started to walk away. "Well, nice meeting you, Ms. Wrath. See you around." Bobb disappeared before I could ask him how he knew my name. I'd never introduced myself.

I ran through the bushes to the sidewalk, but Bobb with three Bs was gone. I walked a few minutes in every direction, but there was no sign of this "neighbor." And what was he looking for in my yard? Was it Philby? Was my cat his cat? I guessed that could be possible. I felt a little twinge of dismay. I was starting to like the fat cat. Well, okay, I was getting used to him.

As I entered the kitchen, I spotted Philby sitting in the kitchen window. His eyes were narrowed, and he was making some sort of growling sound. Had he seen me out there with Bobb? Maybe he was Bobb's cat. If that was the case, I was pretty sure he didn't care for his master much.

It would be great if Bobb was Lenny's killer. Great and convenient. But in my experience, convenience never happened. And if he was the murderer, it was pretty bold to just march into my yard in broad daylight, even if he was looking for Philby.

And if he was looking for the cat, why? What did he want with the beast? And why just walk away? If he was a baddie, he would've tried to overpower me. But if he knew who I was, he'd probably decided it wasn't worth risking me fighting back.

All those things just pointed to Bobb as a suspect. I should've tackled him. Pinned him down and made him tell me what was going on. Why didn't I do that?

Well, because I wasn't a spy anymore, and it was sort of frowned upon to beat up your neighbors when they popped in to introduce themselves. I wondered if Kelly would know him. She lived at the other end of the block and has been here all her life. I'd have to ask her.

The doorbell rang. "What now?" I grumbled as I opened the door.

Another stranger stood before me, this time a woman in a dark green suit. Her shoulder-length red hair perfectly framed her pretty face. Green eyes smiled at me as she extended a precisely manicured hand.

"Ms. Wrath?" she asked pleasantly. "My name is Juliette Dowd. I'm from the Girl Scout Council. Do you have a moment to talk?" After she shook my hand, she handed me a card with the Council's logo and her name.

I stared at her. As far as I knew, I wasn't expecting anyone from the Council. What was she doing here?

"Sure," I said, trying to dredge up some matching enthusiasm. "Come in." I led her into the kitchen and had her pull up a seat at the breakfast bar. Philby jumped up in front of her and sat there, staring at her as if he was sizing her up.

"Is this your cat?" Juliette cried, clapping her hands together. "Oh! I adore kitties!" She started scratching under Philby's chin, and the traitor immediately started purring like a rusty freight train.

"Oooh! You're a big boy, aren't you?" The woman trilled and cooed, and the cat responded by melting all over the counter. He rolled onto his back and offered up his tummy, which the redhead scratched as she giggled.

It gave me a few moments to size her up. Clearly this woman was administration. She had that charm that hid a layer of passive-aggressive meanness just beneath the surface. This woman was disarmingly attractive, but beneath the manicure were stainless steel claws. I'd had experience with this type before. She reminded me of an IRA agent I once knew who liked blowing up sheep.

"Ms. Wrath," she said as she continued to pet my cat. "I understand you've been with us a little over a year, is that right?" The smile vanished as she reached into her tote bag and pulled out a file. A very thick file. *Uh-oh.*

"That's right," I said. I didn't offer her anything to drink. Why should I? She was here to let me have it. I was as certain about that as I was that you didn't give Uzbeks matches. Not ever.

Juliette opened the file and looked at me. All of her charm was gone and replaced with a terrifying mask of hostility. I didn't respond. It would only feed her dragon lady need for inducing fear.

"I'm not convinced we did a proper job in vetting you, Ms. Wrath." Her originally melodious voice had turned to sharp, barbed wire. I said nothing.

"It seems to me that there was an incident recently that caused your troop to be used as human shields by terrorists?" She arched one lethal eyebrow.

"That was all covered in my report. The police backed me up on this. The Council cleared me of all blame." I folded my arms over my chest and met her glare with one of my own.

Ms. Juliette Dowd closed the file and leaned back on the stool. "I know that. But I'm not convinced."

"What is your title, Ms. Dowd?" Might as well get to the point. She wasn't the CEO—I'd met her a couple of months ago when we went over all this. She wasn't the Council's attorney either. I'd met him at the same time. So I wasn't entirely sure this woman had a reason for a witch-hunt.

"I'm the county membership coordinator, Ms. Wrath." Juliette's eyes narrowed to angry little slits. "And I don't like you. I don't like your file. I don't like that I have no information about you before one year ago."

This woman should've chosen a profession in the IRS or CIA.

"That's too bad. Can I show you out?" I asked as I gripped her elbow and moved her toward the door.

She didn't struggle. "Fine. For now." She shoved the file into her bag as I opened the door for her. "But this isn't over. When I'm done, you'll wish you'd never volunteered!" She was spitting like a wildcat now.

"Too late," I said as I slammed the door in her face. I turned around and ran smack into Riley. He grabbed my arms to steady me as I wobbled.

"What the hell, Riley?" I shouted. For a second, my eyes caught his and I felt that little tug of attraction I'd once felt for him and his surfer good looks.

Riley smiled. "So, who's the hot redhead?" he asked.

I was furious. "Not your type, I'm afraid. She's out to get me."

"What?" My former boss frowned. "They've found you already? Who does she work for?" He reached for his cell and went to look out the front window.

I toyed with letting him feel all protective and stuff. But I didn't want him for one minute to think that woman could get the jump on me.

"Relax. She's with the Girl Scouts. I can handle her."

Riley frowned and put his cell back in his pocket. "I thought you were cleared."

I nodded. "I was. She has no authority. This seems to be something more personal. I don't know how, but she clearly hates me and wants me out of scouting."

He shrugged. "Would that be a bad thing?"

I glared at him. "It's the only thing in my life right now that I enjoy."

Riley held out his hands defensively, "Okay, okay. I get it."

"Come on." I motioned for him to follow me. "Let me make you a salad."

CHAPTER SIX

————

"What's in this?" Riley made another face that looked like he was being tortured with a dirty spork.

I swallowed a mouthful of ravioli. "What? It's a salad. I thought you liked salad."

He picked around the plate with his fork. "Are those rutabagas? And radishes?" He looked up at me. "Are you trying to kill me?"

"No. Why? Is it working?" I asked.

"It's bitter and super spicy." He speared a red pepper. "And the dressing makes it worse."

I shrugged. "I thought that's what you wanted?" I dumped a bunch of processed cheese on top of my pasta and kept eating.

Riley put his fork down and slid the plate away. I couldn't help but notice him eyeing my food as his stomach rumbled.

"Just so you know, the local police are turning the Lenny case over to us. They don't want to work with the Feds on this," Riley said.

"So the agency is handling everything? Well that's good news." Now we controlled the story and access. "Have you talked to the prison yet?"

"I was getting to that." Riley gave me a look. *Uh-oh.* "Lenny had a visitor last week. Want to take a guess at who it was?"

"Not really." I answered, swallowing a lump of ravioli that had lodged in my throat.

"Merrygold Wrath," Riley said. "He had one visitor named Merrygold Wrath."

"Well, obviously, it wasn't me," I said. "I was here all last week. I'm here every week. Last trip I had out of town was with you to Chicago to dump Midori's body."

Riley's lips became a tight line. "About that..."

"They found her?" I wasn't too surprised. It was only a matter of time before the body turned up. Three months seemed right. We'd hidden the dead Yakuza leader in the woods behind the Dumpster at an Asian food market. Her appearance, dead in my kitchen, was the only loose end we hadn't wrapped up from the last adventure.

He nodded. "They aren't looking at us. They think someone in organized crime in Chicago did it. We're off the radar."

I relaxed a little. "Which still doesn't explain what she was doing here."

"At this point," Riley said, "I don't care about that. What I do care about is how an inept, former spy escaped from a supermax prison and ended up at the home of a former agent of ours, who lives deep undercover, and who visited him using her cover name last week."

"I didn't visit him." I was starting to get mad. "You don't believe me?" I'd once been attracted to Riley. But his lack of trust was tarnishing that appeal somewhat.

"I believe you," he said with a sigh. "They're sending me the video footage of your visit. That should prove it isn't you." He gave me a look that said, *It had better prove it wasn't you.* "But I'm worried that we need to relocate you to another place with another persona."

I shook my head. "No way. I bleached my hair, changed my name, and am wearing different-colored contact lenses. I'm not going through that again. Besides, I have a life I like here." And I did. Kelly, my best friend, lived here. I also had my Girl Scouts and my boyfriend, Rex.

"I can't make you," Riley said. "You don't work for the CIA anymore. But I think you should consider it. It may not be safe here anymore." He sounded a little concerned for me. That softened me up more than I'd have liked it to.

"That's right. I don't work for the agency anymore. I'm staying here."

Riley looked at me for a moment, with a glimmer of defeat in his eyes. "Okay, but you have to keep me apprised on everything. I'm going to run background checks on everyone from that woman who was just here to Dr. Rye."

"The veterinarian? Are you kidding?" I choked on my drink. "I think it's safe to say he's harmless. Although I don't mind you dealing with the Council's dragon lady."

"Anyone you come into contact with—I want to know about," Riley said firmly. Apparently, he wasn't taking no for an answer.

I remembered something. "Bobb!" Philby jumped up on the counter and began hissing at me.

"Bob? Who's Bob?" Riley asked, his eyes on the cat, who hissed again at the name's mention. Twice. And on the second *Bob*, spit flew. I kind of hoped it was acid spit that would dissolve the counter top. Sadly, it didn't.

"With three *B*s." I nodded. Philby did nothing. He didn't even *try* to spit acid. Lazy cat.

Riley turned wide eyes on me. "Did you say 'Bob with three *B*s'?" Philby hissed again, this time with no spit. He was probably running dry.

I nodded. "Showed up in my backyard just before you got back. He said he was a neighbor, but I've never seen him before. He also knew my name and seemed to be looking for something."

Philby eyed us warily as if waiting for us to say the name again. I didn't, because quite frankly, the cat looked exhausted from all that exertion. I should probably put him on a diet. Maybe he'd eat Riley's salad?

"And you went out there and confronted him?" Riley looked pissed. "Dammit, Wrath! You can't go anywhere unarmed from here on out!"

"I was armed," I snapped. "And I'm not an idiot! I stayed out of reach." How dare he not trust me! Why did he put me alone in such dangerous circumstances all those years?

"What, you took a knife from the kitchen?" Riley's curiosity bested him.

"Sort of..." I answered, starting to regret bringing it up. "I had a carrot."

"A carrot? Like the vegetable?" Riley's eyes grew wide.

I tilted my chin in defiance. "It was a very *pointy* carrot."

Riley threw up his hands in defeat. There was something he wasn't telling me.

"You know him. You know Bobb," I challenged.

Philby hissed so hard he fell over on his side. He looked like a giant, furry tick, wriggling on his side in an attempt to get to his useless feet. I reached over and helped the panting cat. He shot me a look and jumped down off the breakfast bar.

"Yes," Riley nodded. "I know him." He pulled out his cell and dialed.

"Who is he?" I asked.

My former boss covered the phone with his hand. "He's an assassin. And not on our side."

CHAPTER SEVEN

I'd tell you that not much ever happened in Who's There, Iowa, but lately that would be a lie. This small city of 10,000 odd (and I mean *odd*) people was only interesting because of its name. Back in the 1950s, the game show *Truth or Consequences* announced a prize for the first city to change their name. A town in New Mexico beat Peterstown, Iowa to it. So the city officials decided to make their own good fortune by naming themselves after another TV show, *Who's There?,* in hopes that the game show would shower us with honors. Unfortunately, the game show got cancelled instead (and had shown no interest whatsoever, anyway), and our name stuck. Most of us just called it WT, and you'd be hard pressed to find anyone who remembered why we even had this stupid name.

When I'd grown up here, I thought the place was the most boring town on Earth, and I couldn't wait to leave to explore the world. And my prayers had been answered when the CIA recruited me in my senior year of college. I went from the dorm to training at The Farm—the agency's secret training facility. I was in the field for years with Riley as my handler, and I saw enough action to know that it was overrated.

By the time I came back home, I appreciated Who's There for what it was—the perfect place to figure out just what I wanted to do with the rest of my life. So far, I hadn't come up with anything but a modestly quiet arrangement that suited me, until a few months ago when my old and new life overlapped. I thought everything except for Midori was wrapped up. I was wrong.

So, Bobb was an assassin for the *other side*. Well, there wasn't just one "other side." I guess that technically, if you think about it, there are several "other sides," including the obvious Russians, Chinese, and Yemenis, to the more obscure Basques, Nepalis, and let's not forget the Irish (never forget the Irish). The list goes on and on. And Bobb worked for one of them.

I thought about the man I'd seen in the backyard. He seemed so...so...American. He looked like an average, middle-aged white guy, and he had the Midwestern twang down perfectly. If he was from one of the other sides, he was very, very good.

"Octopussy," Riley said into his cell phone before hanging up and gathering up the cat. He took me by the arm and led me to his rented SUV. I went only because I was curious why he was using a codeword. And why *Octopussy*? That was a terrible James Bond movie. And what self-respecting female spy would go by such a stupid, demeaning name? And why put the word "octopus" with the word "pussy"? Did it mean she had a vagina with eight arms and suction cups? Ian Fleming had some twisted fantasies.

I still said nothing as we drove across town to a yarn shop. A yarn shop? I really had to see where he was going with this, because unless he was going to knit me a safe house, I wasn't sure why we were here.

Riley parked the car then hefted Philby as he opened the door to All About Ewe and motioned for me to follow. Inside, the walls were covered with bookcases filled with every color of yarn imaginable. A cute, 20-something chick with a severe black pageboy haircut nodded and led us to the back of the shop. She pulled on a bookcase and it opened, revealing a secret room. She closed the case behind us.

"You have a safe house?" I raged, my anger punching my curiosity in the face. "Here? In *my* town? And you never told me? What the hell?"

The room was 15 feet by 15 feet with a couch, table with two chairs, a huge flat-screen TV, a desk with a computer, a fridge and microwave, and a double bed in the corner. There were no windows, but I did have a bathroom. There was only one way in—the way we came. It was comfortable with soft green walls and hardwood floors. But obviously this was a prison. For me.

"You built a lockdown? You planned to use this all along!" I shouted as Riley set Philby on the bed. The cat yawned and stretched and fell asleep. The traitor.

"I'm not staying here," I said, folding my arms over my chest.

Riley arched one eyebrow. "Yes, you are. I'll stay at your place. I'll bring Philby's things over."

"That's *my* house, and you can't commandeer it! I live *there*!" I don't think I'd ever been this angry at Riley. Even after the time in Nicaragua when he accidentally set fire to my shoes (he was trying to start a fire in the middle of nowhere), *while I was wearing them*. Or the time on the Amazon River when he used up all the mosquito spray on himself, leaving me to turn into one huge, itchy welt. Or the time in Moscow when we were undercover in a seedy bar filled with the Russian mafia and he slid out in our getaway car for a booty call—leaving me to walk through the worst part of that city alone. In January. Huh. I realized I had a lot to be mad at Riley for.

"You don't go anywhere without me," Riley replied. "As of right now, you are in danger. My job is to figure out why."

"If Bobb wanted to kill me, he would have," I snarled. Philby hissed quietly, deciding a full-on hiss didn't warrant upsetting his comfort.

"He was scoping you out," Riley said. "There is no argument here, Wrath. You're staying."

"Look," I said evenly in an attempt to reason with him, "I don't think…" I looked at my cat. He was snoring. "…the assassin wanted to kill me. Maybe he wanted to talk to me? Now I won't be there to do so."

Riley shook his head. "I'm not taking any chances." He moved to the door and opened it. "I'll run home to get some things. This door locks from the outside, and I've instructed Suzanne to shoot you with a tranq gun if you try to leave."

"You what?" He what? "I'm trapped in here? This isn't a safe house…it's a cell! And what about safety? How do I get out if my *shoes* catch fire for no reason?" I hoped he'd catch my meaning. He didn't.

"I don't want you getting hurt. Will you please just trust me and stay here? Please?" He sounded exasperated. "And it's not a prison. There's a keypad hidden in here. I'm just not going to give you the code right now."

I threw my arms up in the air. "I don't believe this! You can't keep me here! You have no legal grounds to do so!"

"I know!" He shouted. I wondered what Suzanne thought was happening in here. "But if you would just do this one thing for me...one thing! I'd really appreciate it!" Riley's eyes were pleading. It caught me off guard.

For a moment, I thought about this. I took a couple of deep breaths and closed my eyes. Riley said he was doing this to keep me safe. Fighting him on it wasn't doing any good. My heartbeat started to slow down a little.

He had a point. I didn't want to die any more than the next guy. But I didn't like being locked up. I thought about rushing Riley and twisting his testicles until he shouted for Suzanne to let me out.

On the other hand, I could use some uninterrupted time to think about this. Riley thought I was safe here, so this was as good a place as any to sort things out. *Maybe I should do what he says...for now. If I have to knock him down later to get out of here, I can.* But right now, I'd go along with him.

"I will stay here until you get back. Then we're going to talk," I said.

"Fine." Riley flashed me a dazzling smile. "See you in a bit." The door closed behind him, and I heard the latching sound of a lock. Fantastic.

I sat on the bed and started to pet Philby. He didn't seem to even notice. I thought about Bobb. Riley thought I was his target. So why didn't he kill me on the spot then? I never knew an enemy assassin who didn't take advantage of any opportunity to kill when he had it. And he'd had me in my backyard with the hedges for cover. It would've been perfect.

And yet, Bobb didn't even attempt to approach me. The assassin even let me know he knew my name. And he told me his name with the spelling that would've tipped me off. Why do that? None of it made sense. Surely Riley could see that?

As for me visiting Lenny in the clink...I know I didn't do that. Well, unless I was under the influence of hypnosis. That has happened before. Once in Serbia, a double agent hypnotized me into thinking I was an Olympic soccer player. And, oh yeah, a man. Riley managed to track me down before I made it into the men's locker room to change for a match. Although I'm sure the Nigerian men's team would've caught onto me before I took my shirt off.

No, I couldn't have visited Lenny. Besides, Riley would have the video footage soon enough to prove that. But someone was setting me up. My money was on Bobb. That would be easy. And maybe he pulled off the Midori murder too.

Still, I had Girl Scout Cookies to sell, assassin or no. I couldn't stay here. That would be ridiculous. And I had a boyfriend. He'd wonder what was up. I pulled out my cell and dialed.

"Hey, Merry!" Rex answered. He was using my first name so he must be away from the office.

"Hi, Babe!" Babe? Why did I call him that? Pet names definitely meant the relationship was getting serious, didn't it?

Rex laughed. "I was just thinking of you."

Yay! He was thinking of me! I guess my use of the name, Babe, wasn't so weird after all.

"Well," I said, "Maybe we should get together tonight. Maybe we could go out for dinner or something?" I was on dangerous ground now—suggesting something other than our usual cuddle at his house.

"Oh, sorry, Merry," Rex replied. "I've got to make up meeting my friend. Remember, I was supposed to meet Angela the other night, but you had that unexpected visitor?"

My heart sank. "Um, sure, okay. Who's Angela again?" I asked, hoping it sounded like I couldn't remember. It was a risk. Either sound like a moron or bypass any chance at getting intel on this bimbo.

"Just an old friend. She's in town for a conference this week. I'll fill you in later—I have to get ready."

"Okay. Bye…" I said, trying not to sound like I was sulking. Which I was.

"Bye, Gorgeous," Rex said. That was something—sort of like a very adjectivey pet name.

Angela. So that was her name. *Angela*. I didn't like her name. An Angela was a statuesque, seductive, siren who never once in her life had to take "no" for an answer. She's probably some high-powered executive. But what would she be doing in town at a conference? It's not like we're a big city, like Des Moines, for crying out loud. Who came here for a conference? Well, I guess we *did* have a Radisson.

Likely story—a conference. She's probably always pined for Rex. My mind started snowballing. I'd bet they were together in college. She was recruited by some major corporation, but Rex wanted to be a detective in a small town. Angela threw down an ultimatum and lost him forever. Okay—that part of my made-up story made me feel better.

But now, she's back! Determined to win the love she once lost! Angela would pull out all the stops too, wearing a skin-tight designer suit in blood red and super sexy stiletto high heels. Her long, exotic, mahogany hair in perfect waves cascading over her shoulders as she sashayed to meet him in the hotel lobby.

I shook my head to clear it. Whoa, this was getting a little out of hand. I had no proof of any of this. Besides, he'd called me "Gorgeous"! And he told me all about this date.

Date. No, this couldn't be good. I needed to do something. I looked at my watch. 5 p.m. Damn. I didn't have much time. I needed to act on this intel.

* * *

"What do you mean, you need the night off?" Riley asked me when he got back. "You don't get a night off, Wrath. It doesn't work that way."

He'd returned shortly after my call with Rex with Philby's litter box and food and a bag of my clothes and toiletries. How he knew what I'd need was pretty weird.

"I've got some Girl Scout stuff I have to do tonight," I lied.

"I'll go with you," Riley said.

"No!" I shouted a little too eagerly. No way was I going to bring him along as I spied on Rex. He'd laugh at me. I'd never live it down. "You would be totally bored. I'll be perfectly safe," I promised.

Riley frowned at me. "I don't think so," he said. "Something's up. What's really going on?"

"Nothing." I shrugged. "Just stuff I need to do. Boring stuff."

"That isn't how this works, Wrath. What part of locked up in a safe house do you not understand?"

I narrowed my eyes. "And what part of you can't legally hold me here, and I don't work for you anymore don't you understand?"

Riley crossed his arms over his chest. "You are not going anywhere until I kill Bobb."

Philby hissed from inside of his litter box.

"Then you are going to have to defend yourself, because I'm going to kick your ass and Suzanne's ass too." I got into a defensive stance.

"Like you could take me," Riley sneered, removing his jacket.

I lunged forward and pushed his jacket over his shoulders, locking his arms behind him. Swinging my right leg, I knocked his legs out from under him and then held him facedown on the floor.

"I'm sorry," I murmured in his ear. "What were you saying?" I got off him and allowed him to struggle to his feet. He didn't look very happy.

"I could shoot you," he said, putting his hand on his gun. "Or have Suzanne bring in the tranq gun."

"Yeah, who is Suzanne, anyway?" Curiosity got the best of me. "And why a yarn shop?"

Riley shrugged. "Suzanne is actually from here. She joined the CIA but quit shortly after training. I've kept her number handy." He smiled.

"Ah. One of your conquests?" I asked. "Poor kid. Do I have some stories for her…" I got up, walked over to the door, and knocked.

Riley tackled me and held me against the wall. "Blackmail? Really?" He backed up, releasing me. I did notice with some satisfaction that he got out of my way in case I reciprocated.

I winked. "What do you think, Riley? I've still got the numbers of a few women at the office who might be interested in some information..."

Riley frowned. "You wouldn't."

I smiled because I had him now. "I would."

He sank into a chair, defeated. "I'm just trying to protect you."

"I can protect myself." Except against Angela's plans to take my boyfriend. "I just need a few hours."

"For Girl Scout stuff?" he asked. I nodded.

"Kelly can go with you then." He decided.

Oh great. Kelly would probably give me a worse time than Riley ever could.

"That's the only way you're going out for a few hours. With Kelly." Riley crossed his arms to let me know he was serious. "And I mean a few hours, Wrath. You get three. Max."

"You can't make me take Kelly with me!"

"I'm doing this for your own good!" he stormed. Wow. I'd never seen him so angry! Not ever. He'd always had this placid, laid-back surfer vibe.

"What's your deal?" I asked. "Why is this so important to you?"

Riley walked up to me. He took my face in his hands, his lovely blue eyes on mine. "You are important to me." I felt my anger break. Was he going to kiss me again? For some reason, I really, really wanted him to. Oh my God! What was I thinking? I had a boyfriend! I had to solve this case and get rid of Riley so I wouldn't have this temptation anymore.

He released me and walked away, running his hands through his hair and straightening a tie that had never loosened. "I'll take you to Kelly's. She will bring you back here when all is said and done. I'll stay here with you tonight, and we can try to figure this out." He looked at his watch.

"I should be getting the footage from the prison any minute now. We'll go through it when you get back."

"Okay," I said, a little dazed. This man had way too much sway over me. I needed to get out of the range of his pheromones to think. Besides, it was time to stalk my boyfriend and destroy the seductive Angela before being locked down for the night by the CIA. Piece of cake.

CHAPTER EIGHT

―――――

"I don't suppose I've told you yet how stupid this idea is?" Kelly frowned behind me. I could virtually feel her frowning.

"Not since five minutes ago," I said, my voice muffled by the clothes in the closet. I was rummaging for my spy suitcase. It was filled with all the stuff I'd ever need in my life of not being a spy anymore. My fingers grasped the worn, leather handle, and I yanked it out, gulping in the rush of fresh air.

I took the case to the breakfast bar and opened it. Kelly appeared over my shoulder.

"Seriously. You should really think about this."

"Her name is 'Angela,' Kelly. *Angela!*" I said as I plucked a tiny camera from the suitcase. It was the size of a pack of Wrigley's gum. One end held a tiny lens, and there was a small button on top. The bottom of the camera was a screen so I could see what I was taking pictures of. There was a tiny LED light for a flash, but I'd be too far away for it to be useful. I turned it off. A light would just make me stand out anyway.

I retrieved a small, velvet bag from the case and removed its contents. The tracking device was a tiny magnet with a super thin wire coming out of it. There was also a monitor the size of a GPS unit.

"What are you going to do with those?" Kelly asked.

I looked her up and down. "Go get changed. Wear black."

"No way," Kelly said. "I promised Riley I'd be with you every moment."

"Fine," I sniffed. "I'll change, and then we'll go to your house."

Ten minutes later, Kelly was sitting in her car a couple of houses up from my house, and I was sneaking up Rex's driveway dressed all in black. My boyfriend's SUV was parked out front, not in the garage, so it only took a few seconds to place the tracking device. I'd just climbed into Kelly's car as Rex came out of the house.

"If we're going to follow him," Kelly whispered, "why do we need a tracking device?"

"Just in case we lose him," I whispered back as I watched Rex stride out to his car and get in. Wow. He looked fantastic. He had on khaki slacks and dress shoes, a button-down shirt and tie, and a navy blazer. Huh. He didn't get that dressed up with me. My throat started to ache a little.

"Get going!" I hissed as Rex started to pull out of the driveway.

"I can*not* believe I'm doing this," Kelly whispered, throwing the car into drive and creeping slowly down the street.

I turned on my monitor and saw the satisfying little red spot that told me Rex was on the move. Kelly's car was the blue dot.

"You're doing this because you love me."

"By the way, why are we whispering?" Kelly whispered.

I looked at her for a second. "I don't really know," I said in a normal voice.

We followed Rex in silence as he made his way to the downtown area. That made sense. Angela was staying at a hotel, so he must be going to pick her up. And if he lingered there for more than 10 minutes after dropping her off, I was going to use the carrot I brought.

Rex pulled into the check-in area for the Radisson and went inside. Kelly parked across the street and turned her lights off. We sat there, waiting.

"She's probably trying to lure him up to her room to seduce him," I grumbled.

"Why would Rex cheat on you?" Kelly asked. It was a stunner of a question. One I didn't think I could answer. Why would Rex cheat on me?

"I don't think he'd go that willingly," I said. "But Angela would pull out all the stops. Men are pretty weak when a naked woman is begging for it."

"Oh for crying out loud." Kelly rolled her eyes. "He told you about it. You said he called you "my gorgeous angel." What more do you want?"

I might have exaggerated what Rex had said to me a smidge. Yes, I'm that insecure.

"There they are!" I was back to whispering for some reason. In seconds I had the camera up and was taking pictures as fast as I could.

"Okay, so she's pretty," Kelly said.

I stopped and looked over the camera. She *was* pretty. Rex, my boyfriend, was laughing as he escorted an attractive honey-gold blonde to his car. Angela was wearing a coat over a dress and high heels. She was grinning at him. He opened the door to the passenger side, and she got in. He closed the door behind her.

I slumped in my seat. "Never mind. It's over. I can't compete with that. Let's get a couple quarts of ice cream and go home to cry."

Kelly started the car. "No way. Not a chance. You finally get a decent boyfriend and you're giving up?"

I stared at her. "What's the point? I make myself miserable watching them flirt all night? I'd rather go home and drive bamboo splinters under my nails."

Rex started driving, and Kelly followed. "No, we're going to follow him so you can see that there's nothing going on. She's probably married, and they're just friends." She had the most determined look on her face. A look I'd seen since we were kids. There'd be no backing out of this now.

"Can we just get ice cream to eat while we spy then?" I asked. I thought it was a fair question. I hadn't had dinner.

We followed them to Trattoria Italiano—the nicest restaurant in town, and parked outside as the two went inside. My heart was around my ankles. Kelly jumped out and ran to the convenience store at the end of the block, returning with two pints of Ben & Jerry's. I loved her.

"What about spoons?" I asked.

Kelly rummaged through the glove compartment and found some sporks. We started eating as the maître d' sat Rex and Angela in a window directly across from us. I really couldn't have set it up any better. We watched as he ordered a bottle of wine, and it was served by the sommelier.

"So why does Riley have you hiding out at the yarn shop?" Kelly asked through a mouthful of Chunky Monkey.

I picked at my Phish Food. "Some stupid assassin is after me." I told her the whole story as we watched Rex and Angela talking and laughing and eating out in a nice restaurant. Something he never did with me.

That struck a harsh note. What kind of relationship did Rex and I even have anyway? We never went out. We hadn't told ourselves we were dating each other exclusively. We fooled around but weren't having sex. Maybe I didn't have a right to think of Rex as my boyfriend. Yeah, so *that* didn't depress me even more. If I was going to get through this surveillance, I was going to have to decide that I was in a committed relationship with Rex. I'd just have to tell him that *he's* in it later.

"How do you get yourself into these situations?" Kelly asked.

I shrugged. "Just lucky, I guess." I set down the ice cream to take a few more photos, but my heart wasn't in it. I was pretty convinced that Rex and Angela were picking out wedding invitations and deciding on the reception venue.

"They're just having dinner," Kelly said, nodding toward the couple. "I haven't seen anything that says otherwise."

"Not yet," I mumbled.

"You need to listen to Riley, by the way," my best friend insisted. "If he thinks you're safer at the yarn shop, you are."

I rolled my eyes. "I'm sure you're right. I just don't want to admit it to him. That man's got enough of an ego as it is."

She winked at me. "Are you sure that's all it's about?"

"What do you mean?" I asked.

Kelly settled into her seat and played with the ice cream, swirling her spork in it. "I think Riley has feelings for you."

I shook my head. "I doubt that. He just likes messing with my head. He likes bossing me around."

"Riiiiiiiiiiiiiight," she said, taking a mouthful of Chunky Monkey.

So, she'd seen something. Huh. Maybe there was something to that. How weird was it that we were talking about Riley liking me, while I was spying on my boyfriend? I felt emotionally compromised. More than I'd ever felt on any mission. I didn't like that feeling.

Rex and Angela were eating dinner. They still laughed and talked but nothing more. *Yet.*

Kelly started giggling.

"What?" I asked suspiciously.

She waved me off. "Nothing." She giggled again, this time a little harder.

"*What*?" I asked.

"It's just..." She couldn't stop laughing. "You. Imprisoned in a yarn shop. I always imagined your life as a spy to be a little more...more dangerous." Kelly started getting hysterical. "I mean, a Turkish prison...sure, or a cave in Cambodia, okay...but a yarn shop?"

I was not amused to see tears starting to pour down her cheeks.

"I didn't pick the location," I said crisply. And I sure as hell wouldn't have picked a yarn shop. I was not crafty in any way. Maybe Riley chose it to humiliate me. At least that's what it was starting to feel like.

"Maybe you can escape by crocheting a ladder..." Kelly snickered.

"Shut up, or I'll make you a sweater," I growled. "A really ugly one that I'll make you wear all the time."

Unfortunately that seemed to set her completely off, and I sat there simmering in silence as my best friend laughed so hard she cried. I ignored her by watching Rex and Angela eat dessert. Separate desserts. On separate plates. They never so much as held hands.

Maybe Kelly was right. I was being ridiculous. Sitting across the street, hiding in a car, dressed in black, taking photos of my boyfriend was a little crazy. Okay, a *lot* crazy. What was wrong with me? How had I become so neurotic?

"I think you're right. This was a stupid idea." I tossed the empty container of ice cream on the floor and looked at Kelly, who had regained her composure but was looking up ugly knit sweater patterns on her cell phone. "We should probably go back."

Kelly nodded and started the car. "Of course I'm right. I get that you're a little paranoid. But you're going to have to trust someone besides me sometime."

"What makes you think I trust you?" I asked, putting on my seatbelt.

"Because I'm a genius," Kelly said dryly. "And you know I'm right."

I nodded. "You were this time." I tilted my head toward the restaurant. "Please don't tell Rex I, uh, did this?"

"And let him dump you? No way! Then you'd monopolize all my time." She winked. "I'm not an idiot."

No you're not. But I sure am. I was feeling pretty bad as she put the car into drive. I looked over to see Rex and Angela coming out the front door of Trattoria Italiano. Kelly and I ducked down in our seats as Rex looked around. Now that I'd come to my senses, it wouldn't do for Rex to see me and ruin everything.

It started to rain, and the two ran to Rex's car. Angela stood behind him as he unlocked the passenger door, and she slid something into his coat pocket. Rex didn't even notice as he opened the door and helped her in.

"Did you see that?" I asked.

Kelly nodded. "It's nothing. Maybe he insisted on paying for dinner, and she was slipping money into his pocket. I've done that."

Rex ran around to his side of the SUV and put his hand into his pocket. He reached in and pulled out something. I whipped out the spy camera and zoomed in, taking pictures. Rex looked at the card, then at the car. Then he got in, and they drove away.

"See? She gave him money," Kelly said as she started driving in the opposite direction.

I looked at the image on the camera and zoomed in.

"First, we need to stop at the nearest drug store," I said, my stomach lurching.

"What? Why? Do you need something?" Kelly asked.

"Yes." What I needed was to get some photos developed. Because what Angela put in Rex's pocket wasn't money. It was a small, plastic card. A hotel room key card. At least, that's what it looked like on the tiny camera screen. And I needed to make sure that's what it was. Before I broke down the door and extracted Angela's teeth and fingernails...one at a time.

CHAPTER NINE

———

"Can I help you?" A bored teenage girl with vacant eyes and limp hair of a color that could only be described as "dust bunny" stood at the photo counter of the closest drugstore. The overhead lighting cast a depressing, gray glow over everything. I'd bet you'd never find the glamorous Angela here. It kind of made me hate her a little more.

"Yes," I said, my hands closing around the mini spy camera in my pocket. "I need to print some pictures."

The kid, whose nametag improbably said *Emmanuelle,* seemed apprehensive. She turned and stared at the photo equipment for what seemed like several minutes.

"Huh. No one ever really does that anymore." The girl walked around behind a large contraption and rustled some papers. She then returned with a book. It was a manual for the machine.

"Do you know how to do that?" I asked.

Emmanuelle looked at me with glassy eyes and shrugged. Her mouth hung open the whole time. I wondered if she couldn't breathe with it closed.

"People usually just print pictures at home. If they print them at all," she said. Every word came out in monosyllable. Lobotomized sea cucumbers had more enthusiasm.

"Well, I don't have a printer," I said simply. "So what do I do here?"

She shrugged again, making me think that confusion was her favorite emotion. "Do you have the SD card or something?"

I pulled out the camera and handed it to her. Her eyes grew wide as she turned it over in her hand. "What's this?" She asked.

"It's my camera," I said, rolling my eyes.

"It is?" Emmanuelle asked, turning it over as if it might sprout a mouth and tell her what to do.

"She's not used to that," Kelly said in my ear. "It's not a normal camera."

"It's the only camera I have!" I protested. But Kelly was right—using a spy camera was probably not my brightest idea.

"How did you print pictures from it before?" Kelly asked.

I shrugged now. "I just handed the camera to Riley when I was done."

"I think…" Emmanuelle said slowly as she handed the camera back to me. "You gotta take out the SD card. That's what we'll insert into the kiosk. I think." Well, at least she *thinks*. The girl raised her right arm to point at another dusty machine in the corner.

"Oh, right," I said as I started to think, maybe for the first time tonight. I twisted the camera and turned, and it opened. I reached in with my fingernail, popped out the SD card, and handed it to her.

Emmanuelle looked at it. She just stood there, immobile, frozen in time. I wondered if she got trapped between dimensions on occasion.

"What?" I asked. "That's the card."

"It's only, like, a centimeter by a millimeter or something," the girl said.

"So?" I shrugged.

She set the tiny chip down and walked over to the kiosk. Emmanuelle wiped the dust away with her arm, then extracted a tray the size of a candy bar. There was a slot in it. The girl held up the SD card—it was way too small. Dammit.

My cell rang.

"Hey Riley," I answered.

"You were supposed to be here half an hour ago!" He didn't sound happy.

"On our way now." I ended the call, took the tiny SD card from the girl, apologized for wasting her time, and thanked her. Kelly drove while I simmered in silence.

"Do you want to go home first?" Kelly asked.

I shook my head. "What for? To see that Rex's car isn't in his driveway? That the house is dark? That would suck."

"We don't know anything," my best friend said firmly.

"No. We don't. I'd just rather go back to the yarn shop and be miserable, please."

"You're getting yourself all worked up for nothing," Kelly said.

"Yes, I am." Might as well admit it.

"You're being ridiculous. There are real problems in the world, you know. People have worse problems than you." Kelly frowned.

"What are you talking about?" I asked.

"Nothing," she snapped. That was a little harsh. I remembered that she'd been grumpy earlier and wondered what was wrong with her. Unfortunately, she gave me the impression that she wouldn't talk about it if I asked. There was no point in asking when she was like this.

My misery was working itself up into a nice little migraine. The stupid headlights in the side view mirror weren't helping.

I sat up very slowly and looked carefully in the mirror, trying not to arouse suspicion. A dark sedan was following us.

"Turn left up here," I said calmly.

Kelly did as asked. I noticed she stiffened in her seat and started glancing in her rearview mirror.

"No sudden movements," I said. We turned left and drove to the end of the block. The sedan followed us.

"Turn left into this alley," I said.

Kelly did as directed. The sedan did not follow. She breathed a sigh of relief as we came out the other end. She turned right to head toward the yarn shop.

The car reappeared in the mirror.

"He's back," I said.

"What do we do?" Kelly asked a little anxiously.

She'd never been in any kind of shoot out. But she was an emergency room nurse, so she'd have nerves of steel.

"Take four lefts in a row," I said. Was it Bobb? I wondered.

Kelly took the first left. Then the second and third.

"Won't he know that we know he's following us?" She asked as she took the fourth left turn. The sedan stayed with us the whole time.

"Yes. But I think he already knows that." I said, never taking my eyes off the car behind us. It was too dark. I couldn't see the driver. Dammit.

I dialed my cell. Riley answered on the first ring.

"We're being followed. Dark sedan. No front license plate," I said automatically, shifting into spy mode.

"Where are you?" Riley's voice took on that same tone. We were working. This was real—just like the old days.

"About five blocks from the safe house," I said. No point in naming it or giving an address, just in case Bobb was somehow listening. For a brief second I worried about Philby. Then I felt a little stupid for that. Riley was with him. I needed to worry about me and Kelly.

"Drive past it. Go to the grocery store up the street. I'll meet you in the freezer section," he said before ending the call.

I relayed the instructions to Kelly, and she followed the directions. We parked and went in quickly. I didn't want to get caught in the dark in a parking lot. Once inside I grabbed a cart, and we made our way to the freezer section.

Kelly said nothing but put two bottles of wine into the cart. I smiled at that. We probably would need a drink afterwards. We stalled in the ice cream section, acting like it was a really tough decision between Häagen-Dazs and Ben & Jerry's (which, of course, it would be).

"So..." Kelly said as she checked the reflection in the freezer doors to see if anyone was sneaking up on us. "What do we do?"

I pulled out my phone and hit the camera function, scanning the opposite direction so it looked like I was just checking text messages.

"Riley's probably in the parking lot checking to see who's in the car. He'll come in and tell us what's up."

We'd played this game before...in Somalia, in Buenos Aires, and at a weird little farmers' market in Reykjavik. It usually worked the same way. The vegetables were a little different, that's all. I liked frozen foods though. You could seriously injure someone using a frozen pizza as a concussion Frisbee or just braining someone with a frozen turkey.

Riley appeared with a basket over his arm. He moved slowly, checking out the frozen dinners. From the look on his face I guessed he'd found the whole section horrifying. After a few seconds of lingering looks at the frozen blueberries, he joined us.

"There's no one in the car. I called the back plate in, but I suspect it won't lead us anywhere," he said quietly.

"Oh, yippee," I said. "That means he's here." I picked up a tube of frozen sausage and weighed it in my hands. It would make a nice bludgeon.

"Kelly, go get in your car, and go home," I said.

"I don't think so." My friend selected two small, frozen turkey breasts, one in each hand.

Riley broke character and looked at her. "Seriously. Listen to Wrath. Go home. Put the car in the garage and lock the doors. It's too dangerous for you here."

Kelly shook her head. "Nope. Besides, someone could get hurt. You might need a nurse."

"Don't be ridiculous! Go home!" I insisted.

"No." Kelly gave me that look, and I knew there was no point arguing any further.

I shrugged at Riley. "She stays."

Riley ground his teeth. "Perfect."

Fffffffffffffffffffffffffffft! A silenced round hit the display case next to us.

Riley and I dropped to the floor, dragging Kelly with us. We knew that sound. That was a bad sound. Above us, a small hole had formed in the glass door, and an explosion of Rocky Road ice cream framed it, which was a terrible waste. This was followed immediately by the lights going out, even in the freezers. Looked like there'd be no ice cream tonight.

CHAPTER TEN

———

"Do you think anyone heard that?" I asked.

"Heard what?" Kelly asked. She spotted the small hole in the case. "Oh."

"I guess that answers my question," I mumbled.

"Did you see the people who shop this late?" Riley asked. "A zombie has more energy."

A bored, male voice came on the loudspeaker, directing people to the main exit due to the power failure. Emergency lights came on in a few places. We heard footsteps and the few shoppers who were out at this hour grumbling as they made their way out. By that time, the three of us were headed toward the loading dock as quietly as we could.

Whoever was shooting at us hadn't popped out to say hello, so we figured we'd just find our own way out. I took the lead, Riley the rear, with Kelly in between us. I didn't care if I was the target—there was no way I'd let my best friend get caught up in this.

Riley was the only one with a gun. Kelly and I at least had our frozen food weapons. We heard no other shots as we passed through baked goods, although I did eye the carrots in produce. Unfortunately all they had were baby carrots—which would take too much time to kill someone with. A watermelon and cantaloupes would work for hurling, but if we could get out unscathed, that seemed to be the better plan.

We passed through the plastic strips that passed for a door to the employees-only entrance to the dock. It was empty. The employees must've gone out the front with the customers. It looked like your standard, boring, cement holding area. Food and other items were stacked against the walls.

"Did you see anyone?" Riley asked as we regrouped. Kelly shook her head.

"Nope," I answered. "And only one shot too. Was it a warning?"

"What kind of assassin gives you a warning shot?" Kelly asked. She was right. That did seem pretty stupid.

"The door…" Riley waved his gun toward our exit, and we crept toward it, keeping low and against the walls.

A silenced shot buzzed by, and the three of us dove behind a large pile of giant bags of dog food.

"Everyone okay?" Riley whispered. Kelly and I nodded. No one was hit.

Ping! Ping! Ping!

Shots hit the bags above and in front of us, causing a hailstorm of dry dog food to shower down on our heads. He'd found us. The exit door was 20 feet away, but we'd be in the open.

"Sounds like a silenced rifle," I said quietly. I looked at Riley's .45. We were outmatched if the gunman was out of range.

"Suggestions?" Kelly asked as three more shots were followed by more raining dog food.

Riley nodded. "I'll run to the left. Draw fire. You two run like hell to the door. Maybe he'll expose himself, and I can hit him."

I shook my head as I rummaged through my purse. "Hand me that broom," I asked Kelly. She grabbed a broom on her right. With all the dog food on the floor now, they would need a backhoe for this mess. I shoved some chewing gum into my mouth and unscrewed the handle from the brush. I motioned for Kelly to hand me her purse, and she did. I found her mirror and using the gum, stuck the mirror onto the handle.

Our shooter would notice a mirror popping up over us. But we might get lucky and catch a glimpse if we slid it along the floor on one side. Riley nodded and got as close to the right edge as he could. I slid the broom handle to him, and he held it out. After a few seconds, a shot blew the mirror to bits, but Riley smiled. He'd seen the shooter. Kelly and I dropped our frozen food weapons and waited.

Riley crouched with his gun, then darted out the left side and fired three shots in quick succession. We heard someone cry out, and I had to grab hold of Kelly to keep her from going back to help. It was a struggle all the way to the door and out into the parking lot.

Riley covered the door while Kelly and I ran to her car out front of the store. A tiny crowd was still standing around. They'd have heard Riley shooting, and the police were probably on their way. The dark sedan was parked a few spaces away, but it was empty.

We got into Kelly's car and drove around to the back where Riley was supposed to be waiting. Where he wasn't.

"What do we do?" Kelly asked. She was panting. She'd handled her first gunfight like a trooper, but I wish she'd never had to.

"I'll go in," I said. "You wait here. If anyone besides me or Riley comes through that door, drive like hell, and don't stop until you get home!" She looked like she wanted to argue. "I mean it Kelly. This time, you'll do what I say!"

"Fine," she agreed. The fight was out of her. She was exhausted and done.

I slipped into the loading dock area and found Riley standing by the entrance to the store, not far from where we'd been hiding. He was looking at a puddle of blood. There was no trail.

"Where is he?" I asked, looking around.

"Not here," Riley said. "And we shouldn't be either. Let's go." He grabbed my arm and guided me outside to Kelly's car. We got in and drove slowly around to the front lot. The crowd was still there, but the sedan wasn't. That bastard had gotten away.

I climbed into Riley's SUV, and we followed Kelly home, making sure she got into the garage without being followed. Then we drove to the yarn shop. Suzanne was waiting, even though the shop was closed. She let us in and left.

Philby came over and sniffed us. Once he realized the smell was dog food, he glared at us and walked away. We were covered in brown, dry dust that itched and stank.

"I know we need to talk about this, but can I take a shower first?" I asked.

Riley nodded. I rummaged through the bag he'd brought, grabbing what I needed, and once in the bathroom, locked the door behind me. It was small—just a stand-up shower stall, a sink, and a toilet. I didn't care.

The hot water felt incredible as it streamed down my face. I lingered a little longer than I should have, but it felt so good. I was exhausted. This day had been a lot longer than I thought. I was too tired to think of Rex and Angela or of Kelly and Riley. My brain was a little fuzzy as I brushed my teeth and climbed into a T-shirt and sweatpants that Riley must've liberated from my room.

"Your turn," I said as I tossed him the shampoo. He already was holding a towel. It was kind of thoughtful of him to think of everything, right down to my deodorant. Most men would probably just bring their stuff and expect you to use it— which I would—but he didn't.

I stretched out on the bed as I heard the shower turn on. Philby came over and sat next to me. His eyes focused on mine like he was trying to tell me something. But my brain was too fuzzy to focus. Besides, he was probably just trying to tell me how much he hated me. I could figure that out on my own.

Exhaustion started in a wave from my legs and arms to my eyelids. The sound of the shower was hypnotic. I reached over to the cat and started scratching under his chin. His eyes bulged, and some weird, inner lid started to close up. As his eyes went crossed, he started to purr. Loudly. The vibrations were making the bed shake.

Huh. Maybe he didn't hate me so much. I continued scratching, and he stretched his neck out until I was supporting his whole body just by his chin. The purring grew louder, and the bed vibrated. It was very soothing. I don't remember passing out. But somewhere along the line, I did.

CHAPTER ELEVEN

———

I was having this weird dream that an elephant was standing on my chest, crushing my lungs. I woke up gasping to find not a pachyderm but an obese Hitler cat lying on me.

Riley was sitting at the desk, typing on the computer. He was wearing nothing but a pair of navy blue pajama bottoms. His blond hair was damp and wavy. His tanned back was nicely muscled and flexed a little as he worked. The room smelled of clean linen. Must've been his aftershave or something. It was nice.

I remembered the last time he'd kissed me back at my house a few months ago. That had been nice too. I remembered thinking he was interested in me. But then, he'd disappeared for three months and didn't respond to my messages until a dead nerd spy was found on my doorstep.

Damn, he was a good-looking man. From his slightly long, blond waves to his gorgeous tan and brilliant white teeth, that man could have any woman he wanted. It bothered me a little that I'd thought at one time he wanted me.

No matter how hard I tried, I couldn't hate him. Or even dislike him. The man was here, once again, trying to bail me out of trouble. I'd had it all wrong. He wasn't bossing me around because he'd missed me working for him. He was here looking after me when he didn't have to anymore.

Ugh. My thoughts were so convoluted. It was more important right now to figure out what was going on. Whoever was trying to kill me had involved my best friend, and I didn't like that.

"Hey." Riley was standing next to the bed, holding out a cup of tea. I sat up and took it, taking a sip.

"Oolong! Where'd you get it?" I asked. I hadn't had oolong tea since he and I had been in Malaysia a few years back.

"I picked it up in China last month." He pulled up a chair and sat down.

So that's where he'd been when he was avoiding me. The scent of the tea wrapped itself around my head and relaxed me. No point in getting into a fight now.

"Who did you see last night?" I asked, sitting up straighter on the bed.

Riley frowned. "A guy in a hoodie. I couldn't see him too well at all. Just enough to know where to aim."

"But you hit him?" I asked, untangling myself from the sheets and getting to my feet. I felt a little vulnerable, sitting in bed with him half-naked and sitting so close. I moved to the other chair and sat down, tucking one leg up under myself, my fingers curling around the steaming, hot mug.

He nodded. "I did. But he got away when we ran out." Riley frowned.

"What is it?" I asked.

"I should've stayed and finished him off," he said.

I shook my head. "I'm glad you helped me get Kelly out of there. She should never have been involved."

"Doesn't matter," Riley said. "The bastard got away." He was taking this pretty hard.

"Well, we know what his car looks like, and we know he can't shoot with any accuracy, so I think we're okay for now," I responded. "And he doesn't know where we are."

Riley sighed, running a tanned hand through his gold locks. "I guess that's something. Still, I would've preferred finding a body instead of a puddle of blood."

"Why did he miss?" I asked. "How many assassins do you know of who miss? I mean, maybe once. Possibly twice—but even that's extremely rare."

"It doesn't make a lot of sense," Riley agreed. "Bobb's never missed a hit as far as I know."

Philby hissed loudly from the bed.

"So maybe it isn't him?" I asked.

"Maybe," Riley said. "I thought it was weird he made contact with you instead of killing you outright. That also goes against his M.O."

"How have I never heard of..." I looked at Philby, who was struggling to get his bulk into his litter box. "...this assassin before? I thought I knew all the players?"

Riley spotted the cat and got the point. He grinned. "He's fairly new. He was starting to make a name for himself right about the time you were handed your walking papers by the agency."

"So what is his modus operandi? How does he usually take out targets, and who does he work for?"

Riley got up and pulled an undershirt from the duffle bag, pulling it on over his nice, lean muscles. I was sad to see him clothed.

"He started to show up on our radar with the Freitag hit in Munich a year and a half ago. Our sources indicated a new player on the scene. We didn't know much about him until he took out Wollan in Oslo a month later."

I nodded—I'd heard of both assassinations. Freitag had been a German politician—a Socialist noted for reform. Wollan was a Norwegian arms dealer with ties to Somali warlords.

"But how did you link those two murders?" I asked. "Neither one was tied to the other."

"It was the way he did it. Always with a rifle at close range. And he left a calling card at both scenes. He cut off their right index fingers in both cases. And he stuffed them into the left nostril of the victims."

"Seriously? This is a grown up? Not a cartoon character? Why did he do that?"

Riley shrugged. "He's never explained it. Over the next year, there were five more hits. All men who had no ties to the other victims. Same index finger picking the same nostril."

"That's how you connected him?" I asked. "From a juvenile gesture?"

"No, we started picking up buzz about him. He's a free agent. Works for the highest bidder. Always goes by the name Bobb."

Philby walked over to Riley and hissed furiously at him. It was almost like the cat couldn't help complaining when he heard the name, and he wanted us to stop saying it.

"Always spelled with two *B*s," Riley continued as he patted the cat on the head. Philby seemed to grudgingly accept this apology and trotted away.

"Anyway, we've never had an eyewitness until now."

I pointed at my chest. "Me. I'm the only one who's ever seen him. Great."

Riley nodded. "You're the only one who's ever seen him and lived to talk about it."

"That seems like a rather odd loose end. Why would he do that?" I wondered. Assassins almost never broke with their M.O. They were creatures of habit. It made no sense that this one would behave differently. I studied my index finger for a moment. I'd like to keep it.

"Have you talked to Langley about this?" I asked.

"I reported it after you fell asleep last night. The license plate was a dead end, but they believe it's him. They also think you're a target."

I threw up my hands. "Great. So not only do I still have dead spies springing up around me, now I have an international killer on my heels."

Riley's cell chimed. He looked at it. "Well, at least we're about to clear you of being at the prison. The video was just emailed to me."

I felt a small sense of relief as I followed him over to the computer and watched him log in. At least there was some good news. I knew I hadn't been in Colorado a week ago. In fact, I hadn't ever been to Colorado as far as I knew. This would take some heat off of me.

Riley clicked on the attachment video, and a new screen opened up. The footage was grainy—black and white—which I thought was weird. Surely a supermax prison could use better equipment. Why was this stuff always grainy black and white?

We could see the back of someone, talking to Lenny, who looked very much alive.

"How do they think that looks like me?" I asked. "It could be anybody." Seriously. This was beyond lame.

Riley shook his head. I could smell the scent of his hair. It smelled like the ocean. "Obviously they were just looking for someone to blame, and you were it. You're being framed."

"Obviously," I grumbled as I focused on the screen.

The visitor was standing up. Lenny nodded and got up on the other side of the wall, replacing the telephone. The camera zoomed in as the visitor turned around...and my face grinned at the camera before moving out of view.

CHAPTER TWELVE

―――

"Well that ain't good," I mumbled as I stared at myself on the screen.

Riley said nothing. And that wasn't good either.

"It's not me," I said.

"It sure looks like you," Riley responded.

"Yes it does. But it's not me." The fake me had only lingered in the scene for a moment before vanishing. It was dark and grainy and the body type was hard to make out. But the face and hair looked like mine. I couldn't deny that.

Someone was setting me up on an epic scale. And when I found them, I was going to kill them. Slowly and painfully. With carrots.

"Now you *have* to stay out of sight," Riley insisted.

"How do I know that you didn't doctor this to make me stay underground?" I asked, even though I knew he wouldn't go that far.

Riley ignored me. "This image will go out to every Fed out there. This town is about to be overrun with agents looking for you."

"Well, good. Maybe they'll find Bobb then." Philby hissed. In his sleep. I really needed to find out what was up with this.

"You think he's behind this?" Riley asked. "There's no connection between him and Lenny, only him and you."

"It's not really a connection," I mumbled. "He just visited and didn't kill me. It's not the same thing."

Riley wasn't listening. He was getting dressed, so I grabbed the duffel and ran into the bathroom to change before he ditched me. I threw on a pair of jeans, driving moccasins, and a sweater, and ran out to see Riley gone but Suzanne and Kelly sitting in his place.

"Where's Riley?" I asked. But I already knew the answer. The bastard was gone.

"He had to go," Kelly said. "I've got the day off so I volunteered to babysit."

"Babysit?" I asked. "*Babysit?* I'm a fully trained CIA operative with years of experience in dangerous situations in the field!"

"Okay." Kelly rolled her eyes. "I'm here to keep you company. How's that?"

"Worse." I sat down hard, folding my arms over my chest to show her I meant business.

"Can I get you anything?" Suzanne asked. It was the first time I'd heard her talk. "The shop's opening in half an hour, but I could run and get you something."

I looked at her with interest. She looked like she'd walked out of *The Great Gatsby*, with her severe, shiny black bob and her red lips and nails. She was dressed in the most beautiful, hunter green cowl-necked sweater over skinny black jeans and black ballet flats. She could be a model. What was she doing in this town?

I held out my hand and walked toward her. "We haven't been officially introduced. I'm Merry Wrath."

Suzanne took my hand and shook it. "Suzanne Aubrey. Nice to meet you." She pulled a business card out of her back pocket and handed it to me. "Here's my number if you need anything."

"The code to the keypad would be awesome," I said with a smile.

She shook her head. Every silky strand of hair fell automatically back into place. "Sorry. I'm under orders. But if you need any help with the computer, I'm kind of a whiz at that."

"Why didn't you try out for the virtual intelligence department at Langley? They need people like that. I always seemed to work with idiots there." That was true. Don't get me wrong, most of the staff were geniuses, but I often got the guys who still worked in WordPerfect and thought a loop was the coolest thing you could make.

Suzanne gave me a tiny, smug smile. "I just don't think it would've worked out. I'm happier here in WT." And with that, she turned on her heel and left.

Who the hell was happier in Who's There? I was only here because I was in hiding. The only charms this town had were the Big Butter Chautauqua and Pork of July. And even those things were just what you'd think they were. The Chautauqua featured every kind of butter you could eat— including deep fried stick of butter on a stick, and the annual Pork of July festival crowned the Pork Princess and Pork Queen every year next to the ever-popular Jell-O Iowa sculpting contest.

Kelly produced a box of donuts and a cup of hot tea. I sat down and started eating. Philby came over and sniffed the donuts hopefully. But Kelly pulled a can of cat food out of her bag and opened it, setting it on the floor. The ground seemed to tremble a little when he leaped down. He tore into the shredded meat as if he were killing it himself.

"So, what's got you locked in?" Kelly asked as I finished off my fourth chocolate donut.

I filled her in on the video and showed her the image on the computer. She sat quietly for a moment.

"So, when you said you couldn't go with me to my nephew's birthday party last week, you were really in Colorado?"

"That's not funny. I wasn't in Colorado, and you know it. And I really was busy. If you must know, I was shopping for curtains."

Kelly arched an eyebrow. This had been a point of contention for a long time now. Mainly because some people thought it was stupid that I had Dora the Explorer sheets as my drapes.

"Where?" she asked.

"You don't really believe I was meeting a criminal at a supermax...?" I asked.

"Where? Where were you shopping for curtains?"

"Interiors by Inez," I answered. "I was asking her how to measure windows, and she was showing me some fabrics I thought would match my green couch."

Kelly smiled. "You know I can check up to see if you're lying."

I nodded. "I know. But I also can't believe you'd entertain the thought for one second that I was really out of state." I was getting pissed. But then, Kelly knew when I was mad before I did most of the time.

She started laughing. "You should see your face! I know you weren't there! It's so obvious that the woman on the monitor isn't you!" She collapsed in a fit of giggles that I would've found offensive had I not been so relieved that not only did she believe me, but she could prove somehow that wasn't me on the video.

"Why isn't it me?" I asked.

Kelly replayed the video. She paused it as the "me" on film looked at the camera. "Earrings. Her ears are pierced. Yours aren't."

I squinted at the screen. It was hard to see at first, but the woman on film had double piercings on both earlobes with a large hoop earring in each one.

"Huh." I traced the hoops with my finger. "Why didn't I think of that?"

Kelly sighed. "Just how did you get through all those assignments without me, anyway?"

I shook my head. "I've got no idea. But I can't wait to show this to Riley. I've never had pierced ears—so that should clear that up."

"What it doesn't clear up is why that woman impersonated you," Kelly said.

"I don't care about that as much as I care about getting the hell out of here. Do you have your car?" I asked.

Kelly nodded. "I'm supposed to let Suzanne know when I want to leave. She'll let me out."

"And you have the day off?" I asked.

"Yes. But I wasn't completely honest with Riley." She looked a little chagrined. "You see, today's the day we pick up the cookies. And I need your help to get them and store them."

"We pick up the cookies before turning in orders? That's insane."

"It is. I don't think the Council has figured that out yet. But we have to pick them up today. I already cleaned out your garage to store them."

"Wait...what?" I asked. "My garage? Why not yours?"

"You don't have anything but your car in yours. My husband and I have two cars in our garage."

I couldn't argue with that. I wanted to though. My biggest fear was that I'd wake up in the middle of the night and eat case after case of Girl Scout Cookies. Maybe I should just pay for the whole shipment outright to save trouble.

"Okay, so how do we get out of here?" I asked.

Kelly threw up her hands. "You're the big super spy with all the field experience."

I looked at the card Suzanne had given me. "Yes, I am. And I'll show you the oldest trick in the book right now."

* * *

"Bribery?" Kelly asked as we drove away. "That's the oldest trick in the book?"

I nodded. "And we got off cheaply too! Only a case of cookies." It had been too easy. Turns out Suzanne had a cookie lust that was easy to satisfy.

I wasn't grinning 10 minutes later at the Council offices.

"Ms. Wrath." Juliette Dowd narrowed her eyes at me. She clicked her pen on and off, like, a thousand times as she looked at her clipboard. Her hatred of me seethed out of every pore. Why did she hate me? Kelly gave me a sidelong glance. Apparently she noticed it too.

"Over there." She pointed to a stack of boxes in the corner. Juliette Dowd leaned toward me. "I'll be watching you."

As we walked over to the boxes, I could feel her eyes boring holes into my back.

"New friend?" Kelly asked.

"More like a fan of my work," I mumbled.

It took the two of us half an hour to review everything, sign off on the shipment, and load the cookies into Kelly's van. It took another hour to unload and organize the cookies in my garage. I grabbed two boxes of each kind, and Kelly and I found ourselves in the kitchen with glasses of milk and a Girl Scout Cookie buffet.

"Heaven..." Kelly sighed as her eyes rolled back in her head. She was on her second sleeve of the mints. I was working my way through the shortbread.

"You're not kidding." I was just opening another box when the doorbell rang.

Rex greeted me with a kiss on the cheek. "Hey! I saw you were home and thought I'd stop by."

It all flooded back to me. *Angela.* The hotel room key card. Everything.

"Oh, hey," I said casually as if I wasn't plotting murder. "Come back to the kitchen. Kelly and I just got done sorting Girl Scout Cookies."

I walked in ahead of Rex and made a face at Kelly. She arched her eyebrow but said nothing. Rex picked the chocolate caramel coconut cookies and started eating. I wondered what that said about him. Maybe that cookie was the number one choice of men who cheated on their girlfriends. I'd have to google that later.

"Where's the cat?" he asked.

"Basement," I said blithely. "Rodent issue." Kelly choked a little on her cookie but recovered nicely. "How was your dinner date with your friend?"

Rex smiled. "Good. You'd like Angela."

I bet. "So what did you two end up doing?" And the answer had better not be *each other.*

"Oh, just dinner. I took her back to her hotel after. We talked a little, but she had to get up early for a seminar."

Likely story. I was trying to figure out how to ask if she'd slipped him her room key, but couldn't.

"So," Kelly said slowly. "Who's this friend?" I wanted to hug her but thought that might look a little weird.

"We were in college together. Kind of went our separate ways after. She wanted to work at a big corporation in a big city. I wanted to come back here and be a detective."

Did I call it or what? I wanted to shout it, but then Rex would know I was jealous. Which I totally was.

"So you were dating in college?" Kelly asked innocently. I really wanted to hug her.

Rex shook his head. "Kind of. After college we lost touch. In fact, I hadn't seen her in eight or nine years when she called up out of the blue a week ago and said she was coming to town."

Ah. That's it. The ice queen was lonely and decided that Rex was the one who got away. Well I wasn't going to make it easy for her.

"How long is she here?" I asked, trying to sound like I didn't care.

"Another few days." Rex said as he took another cookie. "We're going to get together tomorrow night."

Was he dense? Did he really think this wasn't bothering me? Maybe he thought I was too mature to get jealous. Okay. I liked that if it was true. But I was jealous. I'd seen Angela. I couldn't compete with that. My wardrobe consisted of T-shirts, sweatshirts, and jeans—not form-fitting power suits. And my short, curly blonde hair was nothing compared to her long, shiny brunette waves. I didn't own a single pair of stilettos, and I wasn't mesmerizing or seductive in any way.

"You okay?" Rex was staring at me.

From the look Kelly was giving me, I guessed that my thoughts were playing out a little too transparently on my face. Damn. I responded by throwing myself into his arms and kissing him passionately. Not my smoothest move…and it probably tipped him off to my jealousy, but it was nice.

Rex froze for a second then gave in to me totally (which, by the way, is my favorite). Wow, that man could kiss! His lips were firm on mine, and his arms pulled me tight against him. Now he was rethinking our relationship! Time to take it to the next level. I wondered if I'd made my bed. Did I have clean sheets?

"Ahem…" Kelly cleared her throat, and we disengaged immediately.

"Oh! Um, sorry." Rex blushed adorably. "I really should go." He grabbed another cookie. "I'll call you later…okay?" He looked at me hopefully.

"Absolutely," I answered, still in a daze. I watched as the door closed behind him.

"Still worried about Angela?" Kelly asked.

It was like she'd dumped cold water on my libido. Like she crawled into my brain and found the little wrinkly part neatly labeled *libido here* and poured a bucket of ice water on it. I started wondering what kind of signs my brain used. Did it use glitter markers? I hoped not. I'd like to think I was so tough that my brain carved letters in itself. That would be awesome.

"I apologize for interrupting," Kelly said. "But I believe that answers your question about whether or not Rex likes you."

I went to the fridge and broke out a bottle of wine. "Okay. You called it."

My cell rang. Dammit.

"I'm at home, Riley," I said before hanging up. I didn't even give him time to answer.

I didn't have to. He barged in the door and joined us in the kitchen so fast I wondered if he'd called from the driveway.

"What the hell?" he asked, his face red.

"We had to pick up the Girl Scout Cookies." I said calmly, waving at the display in front of him.

Riley's eyes grew wide as he took it in. I poured him a glass of wine and he picked up a chocolate covered mint cookie. For a moment he looked like he was arguing internally about eating it.

"You bribed a government official," he said, but the fight had gone out of his voice. Riley sniffed the cookie.

"No," I countered. "I bribed a yarn shop sales girl who was keeping me, a private citizen, locked up in her back room. Bribing is the least thing I could've done to her. I could've broken her neck, leaving another mess for you." I popped another cookie into my mouth.

Riley took a bite. A small one. He knew what these cookies were made of. But he took the bite nevertheless. I was kind of proud of him.

His eyes rolled back in his head. "This is so good!" He finished the cookie and picked up another one, looking dubiously at the wine.

"Needs milk," Riley said through a mouthful of cookie. I poured him a glass. It was a fattening two percent, but he didn't need to know that.

"While your mouth is full, I should tell you that Kelly can prove it isn't me in the prison video."

Riley swallowed. "I know that."

Well that took the wind out of my sails. I loved proving Riley wrong. It was like a hobby with very few successes. "You do?"

He nodded. "It's obvious."

"You could've mentioned that earlier." I was mad now. He made me think he thought it was me. I snatched a cookie out of his hands.

Riley polished off the glass of milk and wiped his face and hands on a napkin. "You just assumed I thought you were guilty. I thought—quite wrongly it turns out—that it would keep you at the safe house."

"Are you going to tell me how you knew?" I asked.

He shook his head. "Like I said, it's obvious. And no, it's not just the earrings."

My mouth dropped open like a gasping haddock—or at least what I thought a gasping haddock looked like. Did he have me bugged? That's the only way he'd have known about the earrings. Men never noticed stuff like that.

"I'm going to let you mull that one over," Riley said. "Look, you don't have to stay at the safe house permanently. As long as I'm armed and with you, you can stay here. But I'm keeping the option open. All right?"

Kelly and I looked at each other. "Deal." I said. Clearly I'd worn him down. That was nice.

"So who is it in the prison video?" Kelly asked.

Riley shook his head. "I have no idea. And I don't care. Our problem isn't in Colorado. It's here."

"You mean we aren't going to find out how Lenny escaped a supermax?" I was dying to know. Hopefully not literally. I looked at my index finger again and shuddered.

"No. That's their problem. We have to keep Merry away from Bobb." He froze and we looked around. Oh, right. Philby was at the safe house.

"Have you canvassed the neighborhood?" I asked. "He said he lived here. Maybe he's renting or squatting somewhere."

"No. I haven't. But I did bring in a few guys who are going to poke around."

"Who?" I asked. Now I was going to be followed by our spies too?

"Nobody you know. In fact," Riley said as he plucked the cookie from my hands, "it's better if you don't know. Then you won't draw attention to them."

Great. Now we were going to play Spot the Spy. Well I was good at that game. I'd show Riley and the CIA what they were up against.

"So where does that leave us?" Kelly snapped angrily. "We have to sell cookies. I'm not doing everything."

I shot her a look. There was that flash of anger again. And when did I ever make her do everything?

"I'd rather stay here, if you don't mind," I said to Riley. "Can we bring Philby back?"

To my surprise, I missed the cat. Besides, he'd be happier here than in that little room. There were windows here, and he could watch, um, whatever cats watch outside.

Kelly gathered up a couple boxes of cookies. "I'll head home then. Dinner's going to be easy tonight." She left us standing there surrounded by cookies.

Riley and I made a quick run back to the shop to collect Philby, and we were home for another round of cookie buffet for dinner. All three of us were fat and happy when we turned in.

Tomorrow, I thought as I lay in bed, I'm going to finish this thing once and for all. Bobb was dead meat. I fell asleep counting all the ways I could kill him with Girl Scout Cookies.

CHAPTER THIRTEEN

———

Something was wrong. I couldn't breathe out of my left nostril. Oh no! Bobb got me! He's killed me and cut off my index finger and stuffed it into my nose! I'm dead! How did that happen? No one has ever gotten the drop on me. Never.

Wait...if I'm dead, how come I'm worried about breathing? And why is my finger furry? I open my eyes. Yup. Definitely dead. And apparently in hell because Hitler is staring at me. Why am I in hell? Sure, I'd done some questionable things as a spy, but come on, it was in service of my country so that doesn't count.

Meeeeeeeeeeeeeeerrrrrrrrrrrrrooooooooooooow!

Oh. I wasn't in hell. And I wasn't dead. And my index finger was still attached. Philby, not Hitler, was standing over me, his paw planted on my nose.

Meeeeeeeeeeeeeeerrrrrrrrrrrrrooooooooooooow! he howled in my face. Well that was just rude. He must be hungry.

It was still dark outside. This cat and I were going to have a serious conversation on what constituted an appropriate breakfast time. I jumped out of bed and threw on a robe and some slippers and opened the bedroom door.

It was dark in the hallway too. Something was wrong. I just couldn't put my finger on it. I heard the scrape of a shoe from what sounded like the kitchen. Someone was in the house. Was it Bobb? I looked at Philby in horror, but he didn't hiss because I hadn't said the name out loud (although I wouldn't rule out the cat reading my mind in the future).

I looked at the door across the hall. Riley was in there. Knocking would get the attention of whoever was in the house.

Very carefully, I eased the door to his room open, and Philby and I slipped silently inside.

A moonbeam penetrated the darkness and lit a spotlight on a sleeping and very naked Riley. He was lying face down, so I couldn't see *everything*. But that man had a body that looked like it was chiseled out of tan marble. I admired him for, like, a second before Philby head-butted my shin.

Very carefully, I slid the blankets up over his waist and then woke him. Riley sat straight up, pulling his gun from beneath his pillow. That was really a dangerous place to put it. Many a spy had shot themselves stupid doing that. But I'd lecture him later.

"What is it?" Riley whispered.

"Philby woke me. There's someone in the kitchen." I pointed at the door as if that made sense. Then I turned around so he could get dressed.

"Okay." Riley tapped me on the shoulder. He'd put on a T-shirt and pajama pants, and slowly opened the door. I reached behind the door for the large wrench I'd left behind months ago. He gave me a strange look then nodded, and with him in the lead, we stepped into the hallway.

Philby chose not to accompany us. I was okay with that. I didn't want anything to happen to the fur ball. Huh. First I was missing him. Now I was worried about him. He really was my cat.

My eyes adjusted to the darkness quickly, but I knew every inch of my house by heart. I'd memorized it in the dark the first week I moved in because that's what every spy does. It took a couple of days to get everything down just so. Let's just say old habits are hard to break.

We moved toward the entrance to the kitchen and living room. Riley went left, into the kitchen, and I checked the living room. The front door was open. I quietly closed it and checked behind the TV, the Dora the Explorer sheets that were my curtains, and the couch. No one was there.

The light came on, flooding the room, and I squinted to see Riley there.

"No one's here," he said. "But the door to the garage and then to the backyard is open."

I pointed at the front door. "He came in through here. Did he leave anything behind?"

Riley shook his head. "I doubt it. He got through three sets of double deadbolt locks without us noticing. This guy is good."

I installed the double deadbolts the day I moved in. Sure it was a pain, but they were far more effective than the original push button locks. Well, they were until tonight.

To make sure the intruder was gone, Riley swept the garage, basement and bathroom. He found nothing. I wasn't surprised. If Bobb was as good as they said, the house was clean.

"Why didn't he kill you?" Riley asked as we sat down on the couch. Philby jumped up between us and demanded adoration for waking me up.

"You sound disappointed," I answered as I scratched the cat between the ears.

"This is the third time. He tried to kill you at the grocery store, but failed. He didn't even try tonight. Or that first time in your yard. This doesn't make sense."

"Would it make you feel better if I just committed suicide so you could go home?" I asked.

"That's not what I meant." Riley offered a weak smile. "Sorry. I'm just in work mode."

I thought about saying something about how weird it was that he was in work mode in his pajamas, on my couch. And that I'd seen him naked a few minutes ago. I was starting to feel a little like a Bond girl. I kind of wished my pajamas were a negligee and my moccasin slippers were marabou.

I looked at the clock and stood up. "Well it's 3:00 in the morning. I can't think this early. I'm heading to bed."

Riley nodded. "I think I'll just stay up in case he tries to come back."

I said nothing as I made my way back to bed. Philby had decided to stay with Riley so I slid beneath the covers alone.

That was a strange thought. Since when did I feel bad about getting into bed alone? Rex's kiss loomed large in my brain, and then I thought of Riley's yummy body. Who was I kidding? No one wanted to be alone. Hell, even Philby, while it would be like sleeping with a hairy soccer ball, would be an improvement.

Riley's being here was a problem. I couldn't ignore my attraction to him. When he was around I forgot about Rex. And while I didn't know where this was going with the hottie detective, it was further along than my relationship with Riley.

Or was it? I had history with Riley. Years of working together in a job I loved. We'd been through a lot together. But this attraction was new. Before, I'd thought of Riley as my boss. I'd worked with him for years and never felt this way until now. Why was that? What was behind my interest in him?

Well whatever it was, I'd have to get him out of my brain. At least for tonight. If I was going to survive this whole Bobb thing, I'd need some sleep. Closing my eyes, I focused on my breathing until I was out.

* * *

This time I awoke to sun filtering through the shades and the divine smell of bacon and eggs coming from the kitchen. I took a quick shower, dressed, and found Riley frying breakfast under Philby's close supervision.

"Have you been up all night?" I asked. Riley was showered and dressed in jeans and a navy sweater.

He nodded. "Yes. And I've made breakfast." He scooped the eggs and bacon onto a plate and slid them in my direction.

"Nice! And fried food, even." I picked up a slice of bacon. "I'm converting you to the Dark Side. You're welcome."

"It's turkey bacon and egg whites." Riley answered as he started digging in to his own plate. "And fresh squeezed orange juice." He passed me a glass.

I ate it anyway. And it was delicious. I even volunteered to do the dishes. Riley gave Philby the scraps, and he belched happily as he devoured the bits of egg and bacon.

"So," I said as I finished wiping down the counter. "Any ideas on earlier this morning?"

Riley frowned. "Nothing. I called the agency first thing to talk to our profiler about Bobb."

Philby hissed so hard he fell backward off the breakfast bar. He landed on his back and rolled around for a few seconds until he could get back on his feet. We politely acted like we hadn't seen it.

"And?" I asked.

"They don't think it's…" Riley looked at the cat, "…who we think it is."

"It's someone impersonating…um, the assassin?"

Riley nodded. "That's what they think."

"Okay…" I started pacing. "Someone impersonates me a week before Lenny—an enemy spy I've never met, by the way—escapes from the supermax prison in Colorado and dies on my front porch. Then someone impersonates a well-known assassin who no one has ever seen before. This imposter tells me he is the…other guy." Avoiding saying *Bobb* around the cat was not going to be easy.

"This fake assassin—" I shot a glance at Philby, who was lying on his side on the floor, panting. "—makes contact with me to establish his identity as someone else, makes a lame attempt in the grocery store to make it look like he's trying to kill me, but you end up shooting him. Then he breaks in here and does…what?"

"It sounds like that's what's going on." Riley shrugged. "I'd sent a blood sample from the grocery store to the lab at Langley, but they couldn't find any match."

"You didn't tell me that." I made a face.

"It's standard procedure," he said.

"If he's injured, maybe he went to the hospital?" Why didn't I think of that before now? Seriously, I was losing my touch.

"I checked all the hospitals. No one came in with a gunshot wound. This guy repaired it himself," Riley said. "I don't know where I hit him, either. I might've just grazed him."

I frowned. "That doesn't sound like you." Riley was a crack shot. We all were. We'd be dead if we weren't.

"What the hell is going on?"

"I don't know. It makes no sense for the assassin to keep approaching you and failing. If he wanted to scare you, he'd realize it wasn't working."

A strange sound caught my attention. It sounded like an old man coughing.

"What's wrong with Philby?" Riley asked as he knelt down beside the cat that was still on his side but now struggling to breathe.

I joined him. The cat's eyes had gone glassy, and he began to vomit something dark blue. Funny—that didn't look like a hairball. Philby's eyes rolled back into his head, and he began shaking violently.

"Philby?" I asked. "What's wrong with Philby?"

Riley got down on his knees and looked at the animal that suddenly stopped seizing and started foaming at the mouth. This was something we'd seen before—but with people. It was poison.

Without a word, Riley scooped the cat up and ran for the car. I just had time to grab my purse and lock the front door before I got into the SUV as it was rolling backward toward the street. I called the vet while Riley drove. We were there in record time.

We raced into the vet clinic, and Dr. Rye hurried us to a back room. He gave Philby a shot of something and some oxygen. Soon the tiny room was filled with the vet equivalent of cat nurses, before one shooed Riley and me off to a waiting room.

"Besides the bacon and eggs, what did Philby eat this morning?" I asked Riley as a thought slowly turned in my mind.

Riley ran a hand through his hair. "He had some food left over from last night."

"That's what the bastard did when he broke in," I said. "He broke in to poison Philby!"

Riley looked at me. "Philby hisses when he hears the name Bobb. I guess in the back of my mind I thought there was a connection, but until now I never realized it was a real threat!"

"That's what Bobb was looking for in my backyard!" I shouted, my voice echoing in the vestibule. "He was looking for Philby!"

We sat in stunned silence for a moment. How did we miss that?

"He wasn't after you," Riley said. "He was after the cat all along."

Dr. Rye came down the hall toward us, wiping his hands on a towel.

"How is he?" I jumped to my feet.

"He's better. A few minutes ago I thought we'd lost him. But then I heard you shouting, and the cat started hissing and seemed okay. It's the damnedest thing."

CHAPTER FOURTEEN

Dr. Rye told us that he wanted to keep Philby overnight for observation. I wasn't sure. If Bobb was after the animal, he wouldn't be safe here. But then, maybe Bobb thought he'd killed the cat, so maybe it was all over? I agreed to have the vet keep my pet.

"So Bobb thinks that he killed the cat," Riley said after I mentioned what I'd been thinking while we were in the lobby. "And you think he'll just go away?"

"I think it's an opportunity," I answered. "I say we make him think he got away with it."

Which is how we ended up walking out of the clinic with what looked like a bundled up cat. I made a big show of tears. Riley did his best to look sad. Acting wasn't really his thing unless he was seducing a woman. Nothing about a dead pretend cat was sexy, so he struggled a little.

Back at home, I found a box and stuffed it with an old blanket while Riley made a big deal out of digging a hole in the backyard under a big oak tree. Solemnly, we stood under the tree after burying the box. I made a show of weeping and clinging to Riley's arm. He looked pretty serious.

"I don't think I'll ever get another cat," I whined. "It would never be as great as Philby."

Riley just nodded.

"What is going on?" Kelly stormed into the backyard. She froze when she saw my face and the little rounded mound of dirt.

"Oh no! What happened? Why didn't you call me?" she asked hysterically. That was weird. Kelly never got hysterical about anything. I really needed to have a chat with her.

Riley and I swapped glances. This was unintended. But maybe it could work.

"I can't believe you killed the cat!" Kelly shouted. "What is wrong with you?"

Uh-oh. This maybe wasn't such a great idea after all.

"Come inside," I begged. "We'll tell you all about it."

Kelly glared at me. Okay, we were on rage now. What was wrong with this woman?

"She didn't kill him," Riley said. He looked like he was going to bust out laughing. That would be worse.

I grabbed Kelly by the arm, but she shrugged me off. "Fine, it wasn't your fault," she snarled. "But you still should've called me! I'm your best friend!"

Okay...this was getting out of hand.

Riley stepped up and firmly guided Kelly to the house. He murmured softly, things I've heard him say before to distract hysterical women.

I was more concerned that my best friend was furious with me. Why wouldn't she, of all people, wait to hear what I had to say? Granted, the outburst helped if Bobb was spying on us. But I just didn't get why she was going so crazy.

Once inside the house, Riley swept it to make sure no one was inside. It was empty. I poured Kelly a glass of wine, and she grudgingly took it. Once she started breathing again, Riley filled her in on what had happened. After a few moments, Kelly calmed down.

"You still should've called me," she grumbled. There was more she wasn't telling me. But I didn't feel I should bring up her recent mood swings in front of Riley.

"Okay, fine," I said. "I am guilty of that. I'm sorry."

"It's just that I really liked that cat," Kelly said.

"He's still alive," I said.

She ignored me. "I thought Philby was the best thing for you. You two needed each other."

"He's still alive. And I like him too." I was a little confused now. We needed each other? What kind of loser was I that I *needed* a cat?

"We're picking him up tomorrow," Riley soothed. He really was good at this. "I'm so sorry to upset you. We just wanted to lay a trap for Bobb. We're hoping he was listening out there or will come back tonight to make sure he's dead."

I wasn't sure how comforting those actual words were, but that was what we were trying to do.

"I've got to go to work," Kelly said suddenly, standing up and heading for the door. "Call me if something happens." She slammed the door behind her.

"Something tells me I'm going to pay for this fake dead cat later," I said.

"Well, let's hunker down for the day," Riley said as he took out his laptop and set up on the breakfast bar.

"That's it? We're just going to hang out here all day?" I asked. That sounded boring.

Riley nodded. "Yes. We have to see if Bobb comes back to look for Philby."

I looked out the window at the sad grave of the blanket in a box. "It needs a tombstone," I said.

In the garage I found some paint, and after scouring the backyard, I found a large rock. It took me an hour to paint it and find a way to stick it in the ground near the grave, but it worked.

"Philby Wrath," Riley read over my shoulder as I worked in the dirt. "Beloved Cat. Rest In Peace."

"I wanted to write more, but I ran out of room," I said, wiping my hands as I rose to my feet.

"I can see that." He pointed to the way the word *Peace* got smaller and smaller toward the end until the final *e* looked more like a period.

"Yeah, well," I said, "I had to do something to remember him by." I'd wanted to put something about how even though he looked like Hitler, he was actually more like Winston Churchill, but there was no way I could fit that on there.

"He's not dead," Riley whispered.

"I know that. But still, it seems like we should honor his memory." No, he wasn't dead. But when he came back, and if he could read and understand words, he'd feel a little flattered maybe.

We headed back inside and stayed discreetly away from the window so we could see if Bobb returned. I spent the day calling various relatives and blackmailing them into buying Girl

Scout Cookies. My parents lived in Washington, DC where Dad was a senator, and I had a few scattered aunts and cousins, but not much else. And of course, I used a burner phone so they couldn't reuse the number. I kept a whole drawer of them in my nightstand. Spy craft isn't just for spies—sometimes it's useful against annoying relatives too.

"Dad?" I said as my father, Senator Czrygy, answered.

"Hey, Pumpkin! What's up?" His gravelly voice made me feel better instantly.

"Is this a bad time?" I asked. My father was a busy man. He chaired several committees and worked 15-hour days. Mom was involved in probably every charity in DC. Getting hold of her would be even harder than getting hold of Dad.

"I have a vote on the Senate floor in 10 minutes. But I have time for you," he said. I could hear the smile in his voice.

I made my pitch quick, and he said he'd strong-arm his buddies into buying cookies. Apparently, cookies in the Midwest were a lot cheaper than the rates in the big cities. And a certain senator from Tennessee had a serious peanut butter cookie addiction. I hung up knowing I'd do well there.

I was selling, but I could do better. I needed to make bank so the troop could do some cool stuff this year. I could just pay for everything—my settlement from the CIA was beyond generous. But Kelly didn't like that. She wanted the girls to work for their money. While I sat there, I put down Riley (without telling him, because why should I?) for two boxes of each kind.

I needed to put the word out at Langley. The CIA agents who still worked there had serious sugar addictions. It was a huge problem. About three years ago we had agents getting sick in Asia. After 53 were hospitalized we discovered that the Chinese had poisoned several cases of American candy bars (I'm not at liberty to name the brand—it's classified) that had been sent to each division head. I wasn't so surprised they were poisoned as much as I was surprised the management had actually shared the candy with the field guys.

Still, I figured I was a trustworthy person to buy from, so I made a list of the spies I still knew and made one phone call.

"Maria Gomez." The woman on the line sounded all business, but she was actually one of the few fun people at

Langley. She could do this thing with her tongue...it's also classified, but you'd laugh so hard you'd fall over if you saw it. Trust me.

"Hey, Maria! It's Finn Czrygy," I said, using my real name. A name that sounded so foreign to me since I'd had to stop using it a year ago.

"Finn! How the hell are you, girl?" Maria laughed.

"Well, I'm selling Girl Scout Cookies now," I said. "What can I put you down for?"

"Seriously?" Maria's voice shrieked. *Uh-oh. Here it comes. From international spy to Girl Scout leader.* I was now going to have to endure a few minutes of laughter.

"Oh my God, girl! How much can I legally buy?" she squealed. Not what I expected, but that's okay.

I filled her in on the different types of cookies, and to my shock, she ordered a case of every kind. I wondered if I shouldn't up Riley's order.

"I'll tell everyone here! Give me your cell number, and I'll have them text you!" Maria said.

"How about I give *you* the number and instead of sharing it with everyone—you text me what they want, and I'll send it with Riley." I didn't want the whole agency having my cell. What if there was a mole there? Even if it was a burner phone, I still had to be careful.

"You got it!" Maria promised. "Wait, did you say Riley the Hottie is there with you?"

I gave Riley a sidelong glance, and he looked up at me. "Oh yeah. He's sitting next to me at my breakfast bar."

"Tell me he's naked!" Maria always had a bit of a thing for my former boss. I always thought it was in her best interests that she didn't work for him. Or maybe his. Maria was a pretty forceful personality. She probably would have devoured him whole.

"I'll fill you in later! Gotta go!" I said.

"Right. I'll send you orders!" Maria hung up, and I wrote down her order.

Things were looking up. I'd sold 150 boxes on the phone so far. Granted, that only amounted to a quarter a box for the troop, but still—I wasn't making Kelly do *everything* as she'd claimed earlier.

"Was that Gomez?" Riley asked.

"Yes, she's my cookie dealer for the agency now." I winked at him, and he looked startled.

A flash of blue caught the corner of my eye, and I grabbed Riley, dragging him off his seat and onto the floor behind the bar.

"Someone's in the yard," I whispered.

Riley slowly rose until he could see over the breakfast bar and out the window. He came back down to me.

"It's a guy in a hoodie. Same hoodie I saw at the grocery store. He's poking around the grave." Riley pulled his pistol out, and together we crawled toward the door to the garage. A second later, the two of us burst out the back garage door to the yard.

The guy was running as soon as we appeared. He vanished through the hedges.

"You chase him," I said to Riley. "I'll wait here in case he comes back!"

Riley took off running, and I looked down at the grave. The bastard had kicked some of the soil aside. Was he trying to recover Philby's body? That's disgusting. I pushed the dirt back over and had an idea.

* * *

Riley came back about 15 minutes later to find me up to my elbows in cement.

"What...what..." he gasped—was he out of shape? Huh. "...are you doing?" He doubled over until he caught his breath.

I smoothed the cement dome and took the bucket over to the hose and rinsed it and my arms off. I had no desire to allow the goop on my arms to harden, although it would've made for great weapons. *Concrete Arms Girl!* That would be an awesome comic book.

"Come inside for some water," I said. "You look like you're about to pass out."

Riley drank two full glasses of ice water before speaking. I changed into clean clothes and rejoined him in the kitchen.

"I'm not out of shape," he said finally. "I chased him all over the neighborhood. He kept doubling back. I think he actually might be staying somewhere here."

"You lost him?" I tried to stifle a grin.

"Yeah," he said. "At one point he went through some trees and just disappeared. I'll show you where. After I take a quick shower."

"Good idea. We can drive around while waiting for the cement to harden."

Riley shook his head. "I don't know why you did that. It won't stop him."

I nodded. "I know. But it will slow him down. I don't want him finding the cat-less box any sooner than he has to. And I'd think we should notice a guy chipping cement for hours in the backyard."

Riley took a shower, and I stared out the window at the backyard. It was quick-dry cement, left behind from the previous owner. I thought about our runner in the hoodie. I hadn't seen his face. Medium height, not skinny but not average either—more athletic. He ran like he'd done it all his life. That's how he'd eluded Riley.

What I didn't get was why he came back in the daytime. Whatever he'd wanted my fake dead cat for must've been serious. And creepy. I racked my brain over and over but couldn't come up with any reason why an assassin would want my cat dead. It's not like Philby could talk.

Wouldn't that be awesome? A talking cat! One that could testify against bad guys. It would be the perfect thing. And why did spy villains always have pet cats? I thought about Blofeld in *James Bond* and Doctor Evil in *Austin Powers*. They had pet cats. And Philby did resemble a certain German dictator.

I guess dogs are too nice to be evil mascots. Cats are just too unpredictable. That must be it. Why wouldn't a bad guy have a guinea pig or a parakeet? Parakeets could at least talk a little. I once knew a Somali warlord who had a pet parrot. That's how we got him in the end. The parrot would repeat secret plans. He wasn't a particularly smart Somali drug lord. We even arrested the parrot.

Riley returned, dressed in fresh jeans and a black polo shirt. A whiff of his shampoo as he walked by stirred something in me. Was I actually becoming attracted to his damp hair?

We locked up and hit the road. Riley drove the bizarre route on which he'd followed the hoodie runner. We crossed over the same areas so many times I was starting to get lost.

"And then we came through here." He brought the car down a single road that ended in two side-by-side cul-de-sacs, one on either side of the road.

I started giggling.

"What?" Riley asked.

I shook my head. "It's a testicul-de-sack!" I lost it at that point, collapsing in laughter.

Riley frowned and stared at the road. "You've got to be kidding me."

Tears were running down my cheeks. "Testicul-de-sack! Get it?" I pointed.

He nodded. "Yes. I get it. And it is funny. But this is serious!"

"I don't think you get it," I snickered.

"No, really, I do. I'm just not 12 anymore." He frowned.

I wiped my eyes and stared at him. "You're really pissed that this guy ditched you, aren't you?" I hadn't realized he was so insecure. Men's egos are so fragile it's ridiculous.

Riley nodded. "Yes. I'm really pissed that I lost him."

I blinked, my laughter gone. "Huh. Okay. Well, so what? We'll find him."

"I think it was the cookies," he said, staring off in the distance.

"Whoa. What?" I felt the laughter bubbling back up my throat. "You're blaming the cookies?"

He nodded. "Yes. Clearly eating that chemical crap messed with my endurance."

"You're serious?" I asked. "Well you just bought a case of every flavor, so you have to live with that."

He turned toward me. "No, I didn't! I'm not buying any cookies!"

"Already took the money out of your Swiss bank account," I answered. And I had. I just wasn't going to tell him yet. Oh, well.

"When the hell did you do that?" Riley roared.

I shrugged. "You shouldn't leave your laptop open while you shower."

Riley fumed as he threw the car into drive and roared out of the testicul-de-sack. It was an epic moment that I'm sure was completely lost on him.

CHAPTER FIFTEEN

———

Riley didn't talk to me for two whole hours. But that was okay because I started getting a wave of texted cookie orders from Maria. I could barely keep up as I wrote them down. Wow. These spies were serious about junk food. One guy we'd nicknamed Herman the Worm (you don't want to know) ordered 200 boxes.

The crazy thing was how they were paying for the cookies. While a couple had given Maria PayPal account emails and two actually gave credit card numbers, others were giving me overseas account numbers that were clearly not legal. Spies. Yeesh. It took me the whole two hours to catalog the orders and remove the funds. If this kept up, I'd need an accountant.

When all was said and done, I'd sold 843 boxes. Not bad for one afternoon. My troop was on their way to winter sniper camp!

I called Rex, and he offered to take a cookie form to the office to sell for me. He promised me I'd make a ton of sales. I agreed with him because I adored him, but honestly, he'd never measure up to what I'd done in one afternoon. Still, it's the thought that counts. I toyed with putting Angela down for a case or two, but decided against it. *She* didn't *deserve* Girl Scout Cookies.

"One more thing," Rex said. "I'd like you to meet Angela. Can you join us for dinner tomorrow night?"

Join *them*? Like *they* were a *them* already? My mood plummeted. Great. He'd have a chance to compare the two of us side-by-side, and guess who'd be on the losing end of this event? Me. I couldn't compete with that.

"Sure," I lied. "Can't wait to meet her!" I hoped my lack of enthusiasm didn't come through...too much.

"Great! I'm glad you two will get to meet," Rex said. I did not share his excitement.

"So do you want me to just walk over to your house?" I asked. It made sense that we'd go together.

"No. I have a meeting across town. Why don't you just meet the two of us at Selby's Steakhouse? I'll make reservations for 7:00."

"Fine," I said before hanging up. I wasn't going with him. No chance to present us as a couple because we'd be arriving together. Now they were even *more* of a *them*. I was going stag as a tagalong on his date.

If Riley heard the despair in my voice, he didn't show it. Maybe that was for the best. I didn't really feel like talking about it. Instead I just moped around the house, trying not to picture Rex and Angela's wedding...their children...retiring in their golden years...

As it grew darker outside, I turned the lights out in the kitchen so we could see better. It also would make it harder for Hoodie to see us. Riley quietly made us a couple of salads and to my grudging regret, I had to admit they were good.

We spent the rest of the evening sitting quietly in the kitchen, watching. I gave up on worrying about my relationship with Rex and decided instead to focus on the only relationship I had—with my cat. Something was bothering me about Bobb wanting the dead body of my pet.

"I've been thinking—" I said quietly. No point in giving Hoodie Bobb a chance of hearing us too. "—about why he wants the cat. We had him tested for a microchip, didn't we?"

Riley nodded. "Dr. Rye didn't find anything." He didn't seem mad at me anymore, but you never truly know with spies.

"That's not true," I said. "He felt some sort of anomaly and said it was probably just a fatty tumor or something."

"Right. I'd forgotten about that." Riley was paying full attention now. "So maybe there's something *in* the cat that Bobb wants."

"Like a different kind of microchip," I answered. I didn't have to explain to Riley. He knew that the CIA used all kinds of technology that wouldn't be picked up by regular scanning. I even knew a spy in Eastern Europe who hid info inside of squash.

"It could be something that incriminates Bobb," Riley mused.

"Or something of Lenny's," I said. "Let's not forget that the cat and the prisoner showed up at my house at the same time."

Riley shook his head. "Lenny was in prison. He couldn't have had a cat."

I shrugged. "Who knows? Maybe he had it before he went in? Maybe he was bringing it to me for safekeeping?"

"He didn't even know you. Lenny never worked with you," Riley said.

"Well, he got here somehow. He could've picked up the cat after the escape."

"And Bobb was sent to retrieve it?" Riley asked.

"Maybe someone had put a hit out on Philby?" I wondered. "It wouldn't be the first time someone's pet wound up on a hit list. Don't forget that mynah bird in Budapest or the yak in Mongolia." Animals turned up as targets all the time. It really didn't seem quite fair.

"Damn," Riley swore. "That means we should bust Philby out tonight and get him to the safe house." He looked thoughtful for a moment. "I can't believe I just said that. Never in my career would I have ever had the need to say that."

I nodded. "Bobb might come back here, but he also might have figured out that Philby is at the vet's." This depressed me. I wanted my cat to be safe. Wait, did I just call him *my* cat?

Riley let out a long sigh. "Well, get suited up. We're going to break into an animal clinic."

*   *   *

Which is how, an hour later, we found ourselves in an alley behind the clinic, dressed all in black.

"I haven't seen anyone inside," Riley said. "They've all gone home."

"I can't imagine they'd come back tonight. Unless they have meds to give every two hours or something."

Riley nodded. "We should go now. Just in case."

I grabbed my lock picks and climbed out of the car. It was very dark in the alley, which was good, because I didn't want to get busted for something like this. I slid my two tools into the lock and worked carefully with my eyes closed, while Riley kept watch. I worked better with my eyes closed in the dark because then I could focus all my senses on what I felt and heard through the lock. A few twists and turns, and we were in.

Riley closed the door behind us, and we broke out the flashlights.

"Do they have an alarm?" I whispered.

"I don't see a keypad. But then, who'd want to steal animals?" Riley asked. I wondered if he saw the irony in those words, since that's exactly what we were here to do.

We didn't turn the lights on because if someone was outside watching, they'd see it. Our small flashlights didn't light things up beyond a few feet, so we were pretty blind. We were in some kind of room for cleaning supplies, and the smell of bleach was overbearing. There was one door against the opposite wall. That had to be the way in.

We entered into a hallway. I went first and froze as soon as I stepped in. A light was on at one end.

"It's just the lights we saw in the front area when we pulled in," Riley whispered in my ear. For some reason, the intimacy of his breath made me shiver.

"Right. That should just be the front desk and waiting area," I whispered back.

We'd remembered most of the area we'd been in earlier. The building was basically a long rectangle. Reception at one end and the exam rooms down the hallway. We'd guessed that the animals were boarded at the other end.

Still, we checked each exam room as we went, just to make sure no one was still here. We didn't have a lot of time, but we didn't want to risk discovery. Riley checked one room while I checked the next, and so on.

I noticed several cat and dog calendars—one in each room. "I wonder if this would be considered veterinarian porn," I asked.

"Do you have sex on your mind for some reason, Wrath?" I couldn't see Riley, but I could hear him smiling as he said this. Okay, this was a change.

"No," I said as I felt myself blushing. But in all honesty, the answer was yes, now. Riley looked and smelled great. And there was an adrenaline rush with breaking and entering. I tried to ignore my feelings and focus on what we were here to do.

After checking the four exam rooms, we came to a door at the end of the hallway. This had to be it. Very slowly I turned the knob, and together we stepped inside.

The smell of urine, feces, and bleach was strong. I guess I should've expected this. There wasn't a single window. Our flashlight seemed to be swallowed by the darkening gloom, and the room looked like it went on forever.

"This will take a while," I whispered. Immediately a cacophony of barking drowned out all other noise.

I felt Riley's hand on my shoulder. It was heavy and warm. The smell of his shampoo briefly cut through the rank odor. "I'm sure the neighbors are used to hearing this. Don't panic."

I nodded, even though he couldn't have seen it. "So how do we find Philby in here?"

Riley didn't say a word. He just shone his flashlight on cage after cage. There were dozens. But each and every one seemed to have a dog in it. At the other end of the room was another door.

"Maybe this is just dogs?" I asked softly.

Riley's flashlight lit up the door. "Then that must be cats."

We made it through the gauntlet of barking and slipped into the other room. A wave of ammonia overwhelmed us. Definitely the cat room.

Unlike the dogs, the cats made no sound at all. And there were just as many cages in here. The dogs stopped barking in the other room. At least that was good. But how to find Philby fast?

"Do you hear that?" Riley whispered.

Oh yeah. I heard it. Police sirens. And they were coming this way. We definitely tripped some alarm.

"We've got to hurry," Riley said in his normal voice. His flashlight swept the cages but unlike the dogs who all came over to us, the cats remained huddled like dark lumps in the backs of each cage. "What now?" he asked.

I had an idea. "Bobb!" I shouted.

A familiar hiss came from the cage at the end on the right. Philby's eyes glowed as he waited for us to come spring him. Good kitty. I fiddled with the cage latch, and the cat sprang into my arms, which would've been adorable had he not been so heavy. I fell backwards, crashing to the floor with the feline equivalent of a medicine ball on my chest.

"Quit screwing around!" hissed Riley. "We really need to go. Now!"

As I got to my feet, Philby under my right arm, I scanned the room for windows. There were none. Great. We'd have to go halfway across the building to get back to the one door to get out of here. I wondered if the fire marshal knew about this.

Riley was dragging me and the cat out of the room and down the hallway. The sirens stopped. Normally, that would be a good thing. But since they stopped right outside, I knew it wasn't.

We ran through the dog kennel, causing every dog to start barking like maniacs. Well, at least the police knew we were still here. Would Rex break up with me for breaking Philby out of the clink?

I spotted shadows at the reception end of the building, and Riley and I dove into the last exam room. We'd almost made it. Well, not really, but I needed to believe we could've escaped.

"What now?" I whispered.

Riley looked around frantically, but there weren't any windows in here either. What was with this place? I seriously needed to have a chat with Dr. Rye if he was going to continue to be our vet.

We got down on the floor behind the exam table. Doors were slamming in the distance, followed by someone shouting, "Clear!" They were going room to room. I didn't think they'd overlook checking ours. For a moment I actually wondered if we could tunnel out. You know, like in those cartoons where the mouse burrows through a wall in two seconds, leaving a perfectly shaped oval in the wall? Okay, so ours would have to be people-sized and wide enough for Philby, but hey, it was something. No, it wasn't. We were screwed.

It sounded like the whole police force out there. I guess there wasn't much else for them to do. It was a reasonably quiet town. This was like Christmas to them.

"Sorry, Wrath," Riley whispered in my ear.

"Why are you sorry? Both of us got into this," I whispered back. We were crammed together on the floor. He smelled nice—what was my obsession with his shampoo? Philby, on the other hand, did not smell nice. He was getting a bath when we got home. Did you give cats baths?

"It was a stupid idea," Riley whispered back. "I've made much better decisions than this in my career." He sounded sad. I didn't like it.

"I know you have. So have I. You just can't win them all, I guess," I replied softly.

The door flew open, and we held our breaths as if that would actually work. It didn't. Officer Kevin Dooley, a doofus I went to high school with, came around the corner of the exam table and switched on the light.

I sketched a little wave. "Hi, Kevin. We just came to get our cat."

CHAPTER SIXTEEN

───────

Rex did not look happy. Riley, Philby, and I were sitting in his office, while on the other side of the closed door we could see him talking to Dr. Rye through the window. In fact, there were several windows. On an inside office. I wanted to rub that in the vet's face, but decided this might not be the right time.

Riley was on the phone with the CIA, trying to get them to deal with this. I just sat there thinking I'd nailed the last nail in the coffin on my relationship with Rex. Angela won. I doubt she ever got in trouble for breaking in to steal a cat that looked like a murderous dictator. Stupid, perfect, law-abiding *Angela.*

The date was probably off. I'd heard when we were being arrested that witnesses had spotted us breaking in. Great. It was probably some old lady with nothing to do but pursue her healthy interest in conspiracies.

Rex shook hands with Dr. Rye, and the vet left. Rex opened the door, closing it right behind him.

"Dr. Rye isn't going to press charges." Rex said as he sat down at his desk. "For some reason, he thinks you just really missed your cat." He handed me back the vet's phone number that I'd given up when we surrendered. He didn't even thank me for making his job easier.

"So we can go?" Riley asked, standing up. I joined him.

Rex scratched the back of his head. "Can I have a moment with Ms. Wrath?" Uh-oh. He used my formal name.

Riley nodded and left the room extremely quickly. Traitor.

We both watched the door close and the latch click. That was the quietest it was going to be.

"What the hell were you thinking?" Rex tried to restrain himself, which I thought was nice. But there was a definite tone in his voice.

"Sorry." I meant it. "But I've got this assassin chasing me, and it occurred to us that he was after Philby, and we were worried about the cat, because why would the bad guy want him alive, so we went to rescue him." I let out a long breath.

Rex blinked like a goldfish. "From the Lenny Smith thing? You have an assassin chasing you for that? Why didn't you tell me? I could've helped."

I shook my head. "Your captain gave the case back to Riley and the agency, remember? Besides, I didn't want to bother you."

Rex stood up and started pacing. "Bother me? You didn't want to bother me? Someone is trying to kill you, and you didn't want to bother me?" Okay, he was getting a little angry now. I decided to keep silent.

Finally, Rex sat on the front of his desk, inches from me. "You need to tell me everything. I can't have you running around town, dressed in black, scaring little old ladies."

Aha! It *was* a little old lady! Score one for me.

"Okay," I said.

Rex thought for a moment. "You didn't have anything to do with bullet holes and blood showing up at the grocery store the other night, did you?"

"Um..." I said slowly as if it could possibly give me enough time to come up with an answer.

Rex shook his head and held out his hand for me to stop. "Never mind. You're just going to have to add that to telling me everything."

Riley tapped on the glass of the door with a look that asked when I'd get to go.

"Look," Rex said. "I've got to work late to clear all this up. Go home, and I'll call you tomorrow. Okay?"

I nodded and snagged Philby, who was chewing on a plant on the floor.

"Oh," Rex said, causing me to stop. "Don't tell Angela any of this tomorrow night. It's important to me that you impress her."

My shoulders slumped. He wanted to impress her...with his *friend* Merry Wrath. Great.

"I won't." I walked out of his office, and it kind of felt like I was also walking out of his life.

Riley and I were exhausted and decided to just take Philby back to my house instead of to the yarn shop. We smuggled the cat in Riley's jacket as best we could, but if Bobb was looking closely he'd probably know. We checked the house and the cement grave outside but found no evidence of a break-in or tampering. I put out some fresh cat food we picked up on the way for Philby and tossed the old stuff. It was poisoned. I should've sent it to a lab of some sort, but the vet had the info, and it didn't really matter anyway.

Riley kept looking at me strangely. I knew he was freaked out about getting caught. He probably blamed that on me too. Why not?

"I'm going to bed," I said dully as I scooped up Philby and staggered a little under his weight.

"Okay," Riley said. "I'll stay here in the living room and keep an eye on things."

I shrugged and made my way to the bedroom. After placing the cat on the bed and changing clothes, I fell asleep instantly. Misery is a strong sedative.

* * *

The next morning Philby and I joined a fully dressed Riley in the kitchen. He was making breakfast again. I was beyond depressed, so I ate twice as much as usual. I didn't want this mystery anymore. I didn't want the CIA here. I just wanted Philby, Kelly, and my self-loathing.

"Why are you dressed so early?" I asked Riley.

"I'm going with you to your Girl Scout meeting," he said. "Kelly called to remind you."

Oh crap. I'd forgotten. We had a meeting today. I was going to teach the girls how to make weapons using everyday objects. Kelly didn't really like this idea, so I toned it down somewhat. I'd been saving the supplies for months.

I didn't really feel like going. But maybe something like this would cheer me up. We were meeting at Kelly's house in her basement, and Riley was going along, presumably for security. Okay. Might as well get it over with.

Riley was in the backyard, checking on the fake cat grave, when the doorbell rang. I looked through the peephole in the door and opened it.

A man in a trench coat, fedora, blond mustache, and dark sunglasses stood there. "Pssst…" he whispered, before looking from side to side. "I hear you're selling cookies."

"Hey, Abdul. How's it going?" The guy standing in front of me shared an office with me early in my career in Pakistan.

"I have no idea what you're talking about. My name is…Andy. Andy Bellafonte."

I crossed my arms over my chest. "You are Abdul Jones. You like the color red and have a dog named Bubba."

The man shook his head. "I have no idea what you're talking about. I don't even work for the CIA."

"That's funny because I didn't mention the CIA," I said. I wasn't going to make it easy. Abdul never chipped in to the office tea account but drank 10 cups a day.

"I have no idea what you're talking about, Finn," he said. Yeah, he was a great agent. Which was why he was sent back to Langley to work in the marketing department after only six months in the field.

"I never said my name, Abdul," I answered.

The man blinked at me. His fake blond mustache started sliding off. I couldn't tell if he was going to run, cry, or attack. I decided to wait and see what happened.

"Put me down for a case of Peanut Butter Sandwich cookies." Peanut Butter Sandwich cookies—the often ignored bastard of Girl Scout Cookies. Of course he wanted those.

"I'll need the money up front or no deal." I told him how much it would be and held out my hand expectantly.

The mustache fell completely off.

"Um, will you take a check?" Abdul asked as he clumsily pasted the 'stache back on his upper lip.

"Sure," I said, suppressing a snicker. See what I mean? Only a flunky pays with a check with his name and address on it while undercover. Abdul tore out the check and handed it to me.

"Maria will be getting the shipment," I said. Abdul was *not* getting his cookies until his check cleared.

"I was never here," he said, before looking both ways and running away down the sidewalk.

I sighed and closed the door. At least it was another sale.

"Was that Abdul?" Riley asked, appearing very close behind me. I shuddered a little then hoped he hadn't noticed that. He was starting to have a seriously physical effect on me. That wasn't good.

"Yeah." I turned around to face him. How did he get his eyes so blue? "He ordered some cookies. You ready to go?"

"Let's drop Philby off at the safe house first," Riley said.

I agreed. We still had to keep the cat safe. We hid the cat in a duffel bag as we took him to the car. Suzanne at the yarn shop promised he'd be okay. I made a mental note to interrogate her when we got back. It felt like I was leaving my cat with a complete stranger. Sure, Riley knew her, but I didn't.

* * *

The girls were all there when Riley and I arrived. I made him carry the box of supplies. Riley recoiled when he saw the kids. He didn't really have much experience with anyone younger than 19.

The girls thought he was adorable and immediately crowded him like gypsy children at American Tourist Appreciation Day at the Eiffel Tower. Riley shrank back and looked at me in horror, wondering what to do.

"He's got candy in his jacket pockets, girls!" I shouted.

I'd never heard Riley scream like that before.

He really did have candy in his pockets. I'd filled them before handing him his coat as we left the house.

Kelly and I put the cookies on plates on the table then called the girls over for snack time. Riley stood there with sticky handprints all over his clothes, in total shock. I hadn't seen him like that since the night at the Belgian consulate when three of his seducees approached him at the same time. That was hilarious. He walked around with three handprints on his face for two days.

Eventually he joined us as we started the craft. His job was to cut the sides of the rulers so they looked sort of sharp. We couldn't go full out with making a real weapon yet, because they were only second graders. But someday...

I worked on the armband and spring mechanism while Kelly wielded the hot glue gun. She mumbled several times that we should be doing something more fitting, like valentines or tissue paper flowers, but she kept it up.

When we were done, each girl had a secret shiv strapped to her arm. I felt like we'd really accomplished something. Then we got down to cookie orders.

The girls were doing great so far. Many of them had surpassed their individual goal, which was nice considering how expensive the cookies were. We reviewed safety measures when selling, techniques they could use, even emotional blackmail that would work when Grandma said no.

"Mrs. Wrath?" One of the four Kaitlins asked. "Is this your husband?" She pointed to Riley.

"No," I said wearily. "Like I've told you girls before— I'm not married. It's *Ms.* Wrath."

Ava spoke up. "Why not? He's totes adorbs. Don't you like him?"

Riley leaned back in his chair with a smug smile. The bastard. I wondered what totes adorbs meant, but thought that asking might make me less cool.

"Well, yes...I...um...like him...but he's a friend..."

"Mrs. Wrath and Riley, sitting in a tree! K-I-S-S-I-N-G!" the four Kaitlins sang immediately. Kelly started laughing. Riley was still smiling. And I was pretty sure I'd blushed bright red.

"All right! That's enough!" I shouted.

"Mr. Riley?" Ava asked. "Are you going to marry Mrs. Wrath?"

It was Riley's turn to blush, and he did so with purple splotches all over his neck. Funny, I'd seen my former boss in lots of situations over the years that would've given a lesser man a heart attack. But this one almost killed him.

Kelly said nothing. She was enjoying it too much.

"Enough!" I shouted. "It's time to clean up our mess!" The girls giggled en masse like junior Stepford Wives and ran over to the table to clean up.

"Nice save," Kelly murmured in my ear.

"You were no help whatsoever," I grumbled.

She shrugged. So I told her how many cookies I'd sold. Kelly gave a strangled cry and stared at me.

"I haven't even sold one fifth that amount! And I've gone around the hospital twice!" she complained.

This time I shrugged. "I guess I'm just better at it."

"Mrs. Wrath?" asked Inez, probably the cutest girl in the troop—even though I hardly notice that type of thing... "Can we come over and see your cat?"

I gave a sharp look at Kelly. She grinned weakly. "I had to tell them something while I was waiting for you."

I looked down at Inez's adorable face. "Maybe next week, okay? He just came home from the cat hospital and needs his rest."

"Yay" Inez cheered. "Hey, guys! We're going to Mrs. Wrath's house next week to see her kitty!"

Oh, well. Fine. I'd hopefully have everything wrapped up by then. Right? We finished with a game while the parents picked them up one by one. When the last girl had gone, the three of us slumped into chairs.

"How do you do this every week?" Riley asked. "It's like they suck the life right out of you!"

Kelly scowled. "They aren't so bad! I get a kick out of the girls."

I nodded. "They wear me out too. But I love them." Wait. Did I just say I loved my girls? I guess I did. I really did. Wow. A little over a year ago, I would've laughed at anyone (and possibly fired a gun in their direction) if you'd told me I'd have a pet cat and love the little girls in my troop. But I did. Things sure had changed.

"Don't forget. We have the cookie booth coming up." Kelly grabbed my arm as we were leaving.

"Why do you always think I'm going to forget?" I complained.

"Because you always forget!" Kelly snapped. Whoa.

I waved Riley away and leaned in. "What is wrong with you? You're always jumping down my throat lately."

Kelly looked at me for a long moment. "It's nothing. Really. I'm just stressed over the cookie sale and worried about you with this killer running around."

"I think you're keeping something from me. Do you have cancer? Are you and Robert having problems? Are you losing your job?"

"No!" Kelly hissed. "Nothing's wrong! I told you. Now get out of my house!"

We left Kelly and headed toward the yarn shop. Something was wrong with my best friend, and she couldn't even talk to me about it. Was it something I missed? Was that why she's mad—because I didn't notice? Not only was I losing my boyfriend, I might be losing Kelly.

My life was falling apart, but I had no idea why. It didn't make sense. And my night was just going to get worse. I had Suzanne to grill and then a date with my boyfriend and his new possible girlfriend.

"Hey, Riley," I said slowly as an idea swirled around in my mind. "Think Suzanne would babysit Philby tonight?"

"I don't know, why?" he answered, focusing on the road to see if we were being followed.

"Want to go out to dinner with me?" I turned on all possible charm. There wasn't much.

Riley took his eyes off the road and looked at me. "Okay."

"It's me and you and Rex and his friend Angela." I thought it only fair to warn him.

"Sounds good," he said with a grin.

Just for a moment, I thought I detected something strange in his voice. Oh well, it's probably nothing. It's not like he could misconstrue what I'd said. Right?

CHAPTER SEVENTEEN

———

Philby was curled up on a basket full of yarn in the corner of the shop, sound asleep. Suzanne locked the door behind us and turned the sign to *Closed*. I hadn't realized it was so late.

"So...Suzanne..." I said as I scooped the heavy cat into my arms. He stretched and opened his eyes. As soon as he saw me, he fell back asleep. I couldn't tell if that was a good or bad sign.

"I don't know that much about you." I set the cat back down on the bed of yarn. "How long were you actually with the CIA?"

Riley shot me a look. I ignored it.

"Not for very long." Suzanne looked like a bored flapper. She had a knitted cloche cap on over her severe, black bob, and she was wearing a long, vintage dress and mid-heeled leather shoes tied with bows.

"Why did you leave?" I asked. Riley was glaring at me.

Suzanne waved her hand distractedly. "It wasn't what I wanted in the end."

"So you decided to chuck it all for a craft store in the middle of Iowa?" I tried not to let that sound sarcastic, but I don't think it worked. I know I'd asked her this before, but sometimes you have to ask the same question again just to see if you get a different result.

The girl trained her dark eyes on me. "I like the fiber arts. I grew up here."

I thought about that. She'd mentioned before that she'd lived here. I didn't recognize the name Aubrey. But then it was a large town, and I hadn't lived here in a while. Suzanne was definitely younger than I. It was all possible.

"Why did you come back?" She was challenging me. That meant she was smart, which was good since she was watching my cat.

There was no way I was giving her anything, and we were running out of time, so I nodded. "Okay. You passed. You can watch my cat." For now.

Riley filled Suzanne in on the evening's plans, and she agreed to wait with Philby in the back room until we picked him up.

"What was that all about?" Riley growled once we were in the car.

"What?" I asked.

"You know what I'm talking about, Wrath! Why were you grilling my operative?"

I looked at him. "I thought she was just a contractor."

"I vetted her. She's fine. End of discussion," Riley said.

"Whatever." And that was all I said to him as we went home and got ready for dinner.

I took a quick shower and changed into a silk blouse and black skirt. I paid some attention to my short, curly blonde hair, and wondered what kind of disaster the evening would bring.

Rex was pissed at me for liberating my cat in the middle of the night. Riley was pissed because I'd questioned Suzanne. Angela probably hated me because I was dating Rex. Yeah, this was going to be fun.

Riley and I arrived a few minutes early, out of habit, to scope the place. After we checked the bathrooms and found the back exit, we returned to the host's stand to wait for Rex and Angela.

I was having trouble standing next to Riley. He was decked out in a black suit, French blue shirt, and dark gray silk tie. His wavy, blond hair glowed under the dim lighting and he smelled like the ocean. My heart was pounding, and I wondered if he'd spiked his cologne with pheromones. You know, that would be just like him to cheat with science. I couldn't remember ever being more attracted to him. This was seriously getting out of hand. If he was doping me with pheromones, I was going to kill him.

"You are beautiful." Riley grinned. "Absolutely stunning."

Oh, wow. He was really pouring it on tonight. And I was surprised to find that I liked it. Oh, yeah. Definitely pheromones.

"Thanks. You look amazing," I replied, trying to sound cool.

So what did I actually think was going to happen here when I'd invited my former boss? It was all a blur. I think I'd wanted to make Rex jealous. But now I wasn't so sure. I really cared for Rex and was very attracted to him. But he seemed so distant lately. And with Angela in town I was feeling threatened. Spies—even former ones—should never feel threatened.

But now I was spending a lot of time with Riley. And he seemed interested. And he was certainly a hottie who just happened to live with me. Well, for now he did. Riley knew all about my past, and we'd been through a lot together. Only Kelly knew me better. Maybe I should've brought her instead. Although the way she's been acting lately, that wasn't a safe bet either.

"Hey! I didn't know you were coming." Rex arrived and held out his hand to Riley, who shook it. The two men liked each other. But did they suspect that they were two sides in a Merry Wrath romance triangle?

"You must be Merry." Angela stepped around Rex and smiled. Wow. If I thought she was pretty from a distance, she was a serious beauty close up.

"Hi. You must be Angela." I held out my hand and tried my best at an *I don't care at all if you steal my boyfriend* smile.

Angela took my hand firmly and shook. I matched her firmness and held on, my eyes locked on hers. Unfortunately I couldn't seem to let go. I just kept shaking her hand.

"You can let go now, Merry," Rex laughed.

I dropped her hand like it was nuclear waste and stepped back. Riley was using his full charm on Angela. He shook her hand and smiled with his panty-melting grin.

Rex checked in with the hostess while the three of us sized each other up. Angela was stunning. Flawless skin, glittering green eyes, honey-gold hair that shimmered—she was the complete package or a cyborg. The host checked our coats, and I studied my new nemesis.

The woman had a body that could stop traffic in mid-day Cairo. Tiny waist, impressive chest, shapely legs, and the ultimate female Holy Grail—a little black dress that played it all up like a drag queen on a Miami stage. I was doomed.

Five minutes later we were seated at a table near the fireplace. Rex sat on my left, Riley on my right, and Angela across from me. I should've brought a gun. I pictured her falling dead, face first into her salad. The imagery made me start to laugh.

"What's so funny?" Rex asked.

Angela and Riley stared at me. I'm such an idiot.

"Oh, it was just something funny Philby—my cat—did today. Just popped into my head." I lied. Why did I say that? Now I had to come up with something Philby could've done.

"Merry adopted a stray," Rex said to Angela.

"I love cats," Angela purred, making me wonder if she was one. An evil Cyborg cat. "What did Philby do?" she asked.

Riley leaned back and gave me a smile that said, *Now what are you going to come up with?*

I racked my brain. I needed to invent something charming. Something clever and so witty that Angela would get up and say she was going back home immediately because she couldn't compete.

"He threw up a hairball that looked like Richard Nixon!" I blurted out. Now why in hell did I say that? Maybe I was the one who should get up and throw in the towel.

Rex laughed loudly and, thank God, genuinely. Riley chuckled softly. I looked at Angela and felt a blush climbing my neck toward my cheeks. This was definitely the most humiliating thing I'd ever done. Well, this week at least.

The woman smiled. Then she started giggling. Okay, this wasn't so bad.

"Rex told me you were funny!" Angela said. "Nixon! Really?"

"I'm just hoping he'll cough up a JFK," I added. "Then I'll have a complete set to sell on eBay."

Thankfully, the others laughed, and I relaxed a little. One hurdle jumped...hundreds more to go before this dinner was over.

Our server appeared, and Rex demurred to Riley on the wine list. Riley ordered a French red, in French no less. Was he trying to impress me or Angela? Now I looked at her in a new jealous light. Was she going to steal Riley from me too?

Oh, for the love of Pete! Now I wanted both men? What was wrong with me? When did I become so greedy?

We ordered dinner and the conversation turned to the weather and the restaurant—normal, boring stuff. I took this opportunity to study Angela. She might look like a dragon lady, but in reality I knew I could easily take her in a fight. This woman used words in battle, not fists. I started to fantasize about dropping her. She'd probably come at me like a girly girl—flashing her exquisitely manicured nails and employing tactics like scratching and hair pulling.

I'd grab her by her right wrist and turn it sharply to the left, causing her to flip over her own arm and fall on the ground, where I'd step on her throat and squeeze until she tapped out. And she *would* tap out...

"...so interesting, Merry!" I heard the tail end of Angela's comment.

Riley seemed to understand what was going on. "Yes, I got to help her with her troop meeting earlier. The kids are really cute."

Okay—he wouldn't say that normally so he's speaking in code to let me know the woman was asking about me being a Girl Scout leader.

"I love it," I said. I told them all about having four Kaitlins—each one spelled differently. They chuckled over that. I sent a mental thanks to Riley. Wouldn't telepathy be awesome for spies?

We ordered dinner, and I listened carefully from then on. Angela talked about the conference she was here for. It sounded boring to me, but apparently it was awesome to her. Rex had to see how much more interesting I was, right?

Both he and Riley paid Angela a ridiculous amount of attention. I didn't like it. But she hadn't been rude to me. No

Dragon Lady had emerged. She gave me nothing to actually hate her with, damn her.

"Excuse me for a moment," I said as I stood up. I needed a little alone time. The bathroom was always a good spot to decompress and think. Everyone nodded, and I fled. Yes, fled is definitely the word I'd use to describe it.

The bathroom, like all restaurant, mall, and public bathrooms, was located near the back exit as the perfect opportunity for kidnappers. I wondered if psychopaths had a niche market in designing public places as I plunked my purse on the counter and stared at my reflection.

I wasn't bad looking, was I? I mean, I'd had boyfriends before and more than one double agent try to seduce me. I was the same size as Angela, except for her huge boobs. But I certainly wasn't as polished as she was.

Hating her was useless. Even obsessing over her was just going to make me miserable. I'd just have to face facts. Women like her got whatever they wanted. Women like me were "best friends" for guys. That's it. That's why my relationship with Rex was stalled out in Cuddle Land. That's why Riley blew me off for months. I may be fun to hang out with, but I wasn't girlfriend material, I guess.

This was stupid. A few months ago I'd been happy with my quiet little life. Now I wanted everything from the adoration of two men to more adventure. That seemed to err on the side of stupid. Did I really want that?

I did miss my job because I'd loved it. I'd thought I'd be a spy forever. Now I was getting a little action and enjoyed it. Granted, I didn't like the idea of my cat being in danger, but a little cloak and dagger could be fun.

No. I wanted too much. And it was going to break my heart in the end. Time to tell Rex and Riley I just wanted to be friends, because if they both dumped me at the same time, I'd lose it. Yes. That's what I had to do. I didn't need a man anyway because now I had a cat. That's right—look on the bright side.

"You are very pretty." Angela's voice came from behind me, and I spun around into a defensive position. You really shouldn't sneak up on spies. I tried to assume a casual pose by using my fists to fluff my hair. It didn't work.

"Thanks. But you are gorgeous," I responded awkwardly.

Angela nodded and pursed her lips in the mirror. "Rex is quite taken with you, you know."

I stared at her. "Why do you say that?"

"Because you are all he's talked about for two whole dinners." She took out lipstick and expertly swiped her lips.

"Oh. Really?" I asked a bit too hopefully.

She gave me a strange look. "I don't think he's aware he's been doing it."

I didn't know what to say to that. I was still stunned about her admission.

"Anyway," Angela said as she fluffed her hair. "Don't take it too fast. He's had his heart broken before."

"I didn't know that," I said. "I care about Rex a lot."

Angela smirked. "I know. And believe me, the feeling's mutual." She looked me up and down and then left me standing there wondering what had just happened.

CHAPTER EIGHTEEN

———

I was now confused. Angela told me Rex seriously had a thing for me and monopolized their last two dates with me as a conversation point. I analyzed this. She didn't seem too happy about it. And I was okay with that.

Feeling a little more bounce in my step, I opened the door to the hallway and wove my way through the tables. Our dinner was being served, and I was glad because this night was exhausting, and I was ready for bed.

I was just about to sit down when an alarm went off in my brain. Something was wrong. I didn't know it, but my mind did. Something I'd seen was out of place. The sensation of danger rippled through me, and I immediately began scanning the room. The waiter moved away from our table, and I saw that against the back wall, sitting at a table by himself and looking directly at me, was Bobb.

He'd seen me looking at him, but he didn't budge—just winked and went back to his dinner. I slid into my seat and kicked Riley under the table. He looked up slowly, and I nodded toward Bobb. His eyes followed mine and narrowed when he spotted our would-be assassin.

"What do you want to do?" Riley leaned toward me and pointed at my steak to make it look like he was talking about my food. Rex and Angela were deep in conversation about something, and for once tonight, I didn't care.

"Keep an eye on him until he leaves," I said softly. "He knows that we know he's here. It hasn't spooked him."

"Good idea. If he does move, I'll offer to bring the car around, and you slip out the back." Riley said before leaning back and nodding. "Mine is excellent. I could eat here every day."

Suddenly, whether or not Rex was into me or Angela was a bitch wasn't important anymore. Would Bobb pull something here? He hadn't attacked yet, but that meant nothing. I picked up my steak knife and felt its weight. It wasn't balanced enough to make a good throwing knife, but I could use it in close fighting. The peppermill was marble so that would work as a weapon, but again, only in close quarters. I guess I could always hurl Angela at Bobb. Hopefully, he'd be holding a chainsaw at that moment...

Did Riley have his gun? We used to have code words for this so that it wouldn't be detected in polite conversation. But we'd also served together in some strange places so saying things like, "Do you have the hairy, black eels?" or "Are you wearing your lederhosen today?" wouldn't make sense here, and Rex would become suspicious.

We could tell him. He knew we were being stalked. But what could he do? There wasn't enough evidence to arrest Bobb. And he'd probably try to protect Angela, and that was out of the question.

Instead, I pressed my hand to the middle of Riley's back. Oh good. His gun was there. Riley nodded, and I wondered if he too had been trying to make "Are you eating the boiled marmot?" work.

So we had a weapon. I ate quietly while trying to keep an eye on the target across the room. The steak really was fantastic. I wish I could've enjoyed it more, but that was pretty much impossible with a guy who tried to kidnap your cat sitting in the same restaurant.

Bobb made no move to go anywhere. He ordered dinner and wine and just stared at us, which made me wonder if our food had been poisoned or our table sabotaged. I dropped my napkin and under the premise of picking it up, checked out the underside of the table. No bombs.

Our car could've been tagged. The possibilities were endless. Oh, the paranoid life of a spy. Still, it's always a good mantra in the business that when life gives you assassins, you make dead assassins.

Angela's laugh brought me back to the reality that we were at a dinner party. Rex was staring at me oddly. What happened?

"You said that?" he asked me.

I looked from him to Angela, who now had a very smug expression on her face. Uh-oh. Riley gave me an imperceptible headshake. He'd missed it too. Damn.

"I'm sorry," I said quickly. "I missed that. What did I say?" A major lesson of spy craft—don't try to pretend you'd been listening. Embarrassment now is better than *dead* later.

Rex opened his mouth to speak then closed it. Angela gloated. Uh-oh. Whatever it was I'm supposed to have said was really bad.

"You told Angela that she and I made a great couple?" Rex looked hurt. Angela looked like a conniving jackal.

Oh, she was going down now! "Wait! I..."

"Merry? Merry Wrath? Is that really you?" Bobb loomed over the table. Because of Angela, I never saw him sneak up on us. I hoped if he killed any of us, he'd kill her first.

Riley was completely on guard. Apparently he'd missed it too.

I slid my chair back to give me room to pounce if I needed too. "Um, I'm sorry, have we met?" I asked. He was still only inches away from me, and I had no idea what he planned to do.

"We went to high school together! Same year. I had algebra with you." Bobb looked at me earnestly.

"Oh...yeah..." I tried to look like I was struggling with the memory as I got to my feet and held out my hand. "Bobb, isn't it? Sorry. I can't remember your last name."

He took hold of my hand and shook it twice, dropping it quickly. "That's right. And it's Andrews." He gave a quick look at Riley, whose last name, not coincidentally, was Andrews. Bobb knew who both of us were. That wasn't good.

"Well, you folks have a nice dinner. I didn't mean to interrupt." Bobb nodded and left.

"Excuse me." Riley stood and went toward the bathroom in the back. He was going to get the car. Since we were still eating, I'd have to stay here and wait for him to come back. Great.

Rex's eyes followed him, then looked back toward where Bobb had gone.

"Is everything all right?" Rex asked me.

No, everything was not all right. A bad guy just escaped. My date left to follow him. My boyfriend thought I was playing matchmaker with him and his old girlfriend, and I still had steak on my plate and no time to finish it!

"It's fine." I forced a smile and looked at my cell. *Following target* was the message he'd just sent. "Although I think Riley will be a little while."

Rex frowned. Something was up, and he knew it. "Angela—would you see if you could find the waiter and ask for our check?"

As Angela got up to go search, he leaned in close. "What was that all about?"

"Okay, I'll tell you. But first, about what Angela said..."

Rex held up a hand. "We'll talk about that later. Who's Bobb?"

I really, really wanted to tell him about how his friend was a lying, manipulative bitch, but we were running out of time. Angela was pointing to our table. She'd be back any second.

"That's the guy who broke into my house and tried to kidnap Philby." There wasn't any point in lying to Rex. He was a detective. If I didn't tell him, he'd figure it out.

"The assassin? That's him? Why didn't you tell me?"

"Oh right." I snorted. "I should've introduced him to the table as the man who might be trying to kill me and my cat. That would've gone over big."

Angela returned with the waiter, and he set the check on the table. I scooped it up. I felt a little responsible for the way things had played out here.

"I've got this." I said, handing it back to the waiter with my credit card and trying not to "accidentally" throw my knife at Rex's bimbo.

"I'm going to run Angela back to the hotel," Rex said. He didn't look happy. "I'll call you," he said to me.

"It was a pleasure meeting you, Merry," Angela oozed.

"Nice meeting you too," I said but in no way meant.

I watched sadly as the two of them left the restaurant. While waiting for my receipt, I drank the rest of the wine. And not just mine. It helped. A little.

Riley texted minutes later. He'd lost Bobb and was coming back for me. I waited outside, and when Riley pulled up, I got into his SUV.

"What happened?" I asked.

"He raced a train and got across the tracks just before it blew through. He was long gone when the train had fully passed." He sounded as dejected as me.

"That sucks," I said.

"It really does." Riley answered as he drove us to my house.

"Suzanne is going to stay overnight. I didn't want to lead Bobb there. He already knows where you live," Riley said.

I nodded. "Fine." We pulled up into my garage and went inside. Riley swept the house, and I poured two glasses of wine.

"That was a strange dinner." Riley said when he'd joined me. He accepted the wine without question and drank half of it.

I didn't want to talk about Rex or Angela. Especially not with Riley.

"Why did Bobb come up to us like that?" I wondered. "Seems like if he wanted to kill us, he could've any number of times."

"It doesn't make sense," Riley agreed. "Bobb wants us to know he's here. Maybe he thinks intimidation will get us to hand Philby over?"

"Have you found any connection between him and Lenny Smith?" I asked. "There has to be something that ties this all together."

"I haven't found anything yet. But I was wondering if there's a connection to Midori."

I looked at him. "Midori?"

He shrugged. "We never found out why Midori was dead in your kitchen a few months ago."

"Lenny sold secrets. Maybe Bobb was the go-between?" I asked. "It's not a stretch to think the Japanese Yakuza would hire someone like Bobb. And Bobb knows who I am and where I live. Maybe he's just killing two birds with one stone by killing her and Lenny."

"What would the Yakuza want with Lenny? I could see the Japanese government going after technology intel, but the Yakuza?" Riley shook his head. "Besides, the Yakuza only hires Japanese hitmen. They wouldn't even think of hiring this guy."

"There has to be a connection between Bobb, Lenny, and Philby," I mused. "Lenny and the cat showed up at the same time. Bobb a few days later, looking for Philby."

"Bobb must've coordinated the prison break and framed you with the visitor's log and video. It's fairly easy to do."

I shrugged. "But why set me up? I didn't know Lenny or Bobb."

"Somehow, there is a connection to you. I just don't know why, or what it is." Riley drained his glass. "And I don't like it."

"Yeah," I snorted. "You and me both. You know—I thought retirement would be a lot quieter than this." I finished my glass and put both of them in the sink. I was a little tipsy and staggered a little.

Riley caught me in his arms. But instead of letting me go, he pulled me closer to him. I looked up at his face. I couldn't read it.

"I don't want anything to happen to you," he said before his lips came down onto mine.

I was going to reply that I didn't want anything to happen to me either, but I couldn't. Okay, I didn't want to. The room was spinning, and Riley's lips were so firm against mine that I pretty much stopped thinking altogether.

I kissed him back. It was so easy to give in. Riley's lips started a tingling in certain places, and I was lost in his touch. Oh, man! *This is what I've been missing!* I loved kissing Rex too, but Riley's kisses told me he wanted to take this to the next level...*now.* And my body was definitely responding to it. I needed a little attention, dammit!

Things were getting pretty hot and heavy. Hands were starting to roam and a little moaning was going on. It was so good that we nearly missed the muffled crack of a silenced rifle as a bullet whizzed past our heads.

Riley and I dropped to the floor and crawled to the other side of the breakfast bar. Five more shots rang out in quick succession. Bobb couldn't see us, so why was he still shooting? Everything this guy did didn't make sense. If he really wanted to kill us, why didn't he just do it at the restaurant? He was a terrible assassin. And this was in direct conflict with his record.

"It's coming from the backyard," Riley whispered, pulling his .45 from his waistband.

"I hear something else though." I held onto his arms so he couldn't run off. Closing my eyes, I concentrated on the sound.

"He's laying covering fire!" I said. "He's chopping up the cement!" So Bobb was just shooting to keep us from coming outside to stop him from taking my fake dead cat's body.

Four more silenced shots plugged into the wall overhead. The bastard was seriously shooting up my kitchen. I was glad Philby was at the safe house.

"I'm going out through the front to loop around," Riley said. "You stay here."

"But I can help," I protested.

Riley responded by kissing me one more time. "I insist."

I watched in surprise as he snuck out of the kitchen. The door shut quietly behind him, and I wondered what I should do. My gun was downstairs in the basement, so I didn't really have time to retrieve it. Then I remembered that I had my throwing knives in the kitchen. It took only a second to reach up into the drawer and grab them.

Slowly, I crept out into the garage and cracked the door to the yard open a little. Bobb was there, in a hoodie. With one hand, he was firing the rifle into the house, while with the other hand he was hitting the concrete with a small sledgehammer. He looked ridiculous but was actually making a little headway.

And while I didn't mind his grave robbing that much since all that was there was an old blanket, I seriously took offense to the whole shooting of my house thing. I didn't see Riley yet, but he had to be there somewhere.

Should I wait for him to handle it? That really wasn't my style. I was just about to go through the side window when a shot rang out from the yard. I ran back to the door and flung it open, ready to throw a knife once I'd spotted the target.

Riley stood there in the center of the yard. Bobb was gone. But he'd left a puddle of blood on the cracked cement.

I walked over to join him just as Rex came tearing through my shrubs, gun drawn, holding his badge in the other hand. He stopped when he saw me and Riley. Riley reached down and mopped up the blood with a handkerchief as Rex ran over to me.

"Are you two alright?" he asked. He wasn't even out of breath.

I nodded. "Someone took shots at us."

"The assassin who interrupted dinner?" Rex asked. Actually, that would make a great title for a book.

The moon came out from behind a cloud and illuminated the three of us in a silver spotlight.

"I guess that's not all he interrupted," I said, as I pointed to the imprint of red lips on the collar of Rex's shirt.

CHAPTER NINETEEN

———

We were drowned out by the sirens of what seemed to be the entire police department surrounding my house. Riley and I went in through the garage and let Rex in the front door.

Rex sent the patrol cars away and sat down with Riley and me in the living room. He ran his hands through his hair as if trying to figure out what to say. I wondered if he'd address the situation or the lipstick.

I decided to fill him in on what had been happening. It was long overdue. Riley ended the story by saying that the CIA was handling the investigation.

"I get that this is an agency issue..." Rex began. "But we can't have you breaking in wherever you want and holding shootouts in family neighborhoods and grocery stores."

Riley nodded. "I'm sorry. I wasn't thinking."

What? Riley was apologizing? And taking all the blame?

"I'm only going to let you have this one more time," Rex said. "I can report that a gun went off accidentally. But you'll have to promise me you won't fire that in public anymore."

"Absolutely," Riley swore.

"And next time your assassin shows up, let me know, and we'll bring him in," Rex insisted.

"You won't have to," Riley said. "Because he'll be in our custody or dead."

Rex narrowed his eyes. "Then do it outside city limits, because I don't want any more trouble."

The two men went a little cowboy, and I was fearing for a *High Noon* sort of standoff in the living room. Which was kind of sexy. But I was exhausted beyond words, and I wanted all drama gone. I wanted to go to bed and blot out the memories of

Angela's betrayal at the restaurant, her lipstick on Rex's collar, and dumbasses shooting up my house.

"Knock it off, you two," I said, getting between them. "Rex, go home. I promise there won't be any more shooting tonight."

Rex gave me a pained look, but nodded. I waited until he was gone to talk to Riley.

"And you! How could you let him get away again? You seriously need some range time because your shots are way off."

Riley smiled. "What makes you think I let him get away?" He disappeared into the kitchen, and I followed him out to the backyard. Between the shed and hedges at the back corner of the yard, he dragged out our shooter's body. The hood still obscured the face.

"You got him? You got Bobb?" I stammered.

"Yup. I just didn't want the cops to have him." Riley knelt down and pulled the hood back, only to reveal a full ski mask.

I pulled the mask off and jumped backward. "Oh no!"

Riley stood up, frowning at the body. He shook his head as if it would change the circumstances.

"It's Angela!" I gasped. "You shot Angela!"

CHAPTER TWENTY

———

"Is she dead?" I asked as Kelly examined the woman on my kitchen floor. I'd called her, and she arrived in seconds. Whether she was still pissed at me or not didn't matter when there was someone bleeding on my kitchen floor.

"No. But I think she's in a coma. She really should go to the hospital."

"But Kelly! It's *Angela*! And she was *shooting* at us! And she tried to kidnap Philby!" I whined. "Maybe she'll die accidentally? Or maybe she's even brain dead?" A girl can hope.

Kelly shook her head. "I know you're thrilled with this outcome, but as a nurse, I feel she should get medical care, no matter who she is."

I stomped around my kitchen in full tantrum mode while Kelly probed the gunshot wound. Riley had hit her in the shoulder, but the bullet went straight through, weirdly hitting nothing. I figured Kelly would stitch up both holes and we could then have her...possibly for a human sacrifice.

"You're enjoying this." Kelly looked over her bifocals at me. She didn't need them but liked to use the glasses for needlework. I guess this qualified.

"Yes I am. You should've heard what that bitch said at dinner." I folded my arms across my chest like that actually proved something.

Riley was on the phone with Langley. He wanted to make sure the blood sample on his handkerchief would be compared to the blood sample in the grocery store.

"What did she say?" Kelly asked, pausing with her needle in midair.

I told her about the encounter in the bathroom, what she'd said at the table, and about the lipstick on Rex's collar. I'm not sure if it was my imagination or not, but it looked like Kelly was rather fiercely punching the needle through Angela's skin after that.

"Langley's sending a medical team from Chicago. They'll take her to a hospital under our control and analyze the sample," Riley said.

I was only half listening because I was taking pictures of Angela with my spy camera.

"Why don't you have a real camera?" Riley asked.

"I'll get one tomorrow." I said as I clicked the shutter a couple more times. "When will they be here?"

"In half an hour," he said.

I looked up. "It takes two and a half hours to get here from Chicago."

Kelly muttered, "Oh, so you *are* worried about her well-being?"

I shook my head. "No. I just hoped I could run out and pick up a camera and take some more pictures before they got here." I thought they'd make a nice 8x10 to shove under my cheating boyfriend's nose.

"They're flying," Riley said. "We'll have to take her to the airport."

"Well, can I pick up a camera along the way?" I asked, now using my cell phone to take selfies of me smiling next to comatose Angela.

"Stop that!" Kelly swatted me away.

"No. We have to go in 10 minutes. As soon as Kelly's done stitching her up."

I pouted. It's not every day that your nemesis turns out to be an assassin. You had to celebrate moments like this.

Kelly finished both stitches and helped us take Angela out to the garage to put in Riley's SUV. We drove to the airport, and Riley got us to the private hangars with his badge. A small private plane with two EMTs took Angela away.

"I don't remember those bruises on her face..." Kelly murmured.

"That's weird," I lied. "I don't either." Okay...okay, I might've accidentally hit her face on the doorframe to the garage once or five times...

We stopped at the yarn shop and picked up Philby, who seemed happy to see me or constipated. When we arrived home, Kelly had to leave. She was working third shift. She reminded me yet again that I owed her before she walked out the door.

I sat on the couch with Philby while Riley brought us two glasses of wine. He started to set it on the coffee table, but after studying the crooked mess I'd made putting it together, decided the glasses were safer in our hands. Philby sat between us and purred.

"So Angela is the assassin? She must've impersonated me at the prison. It's pretty easy to fake a video," I said as I pet my cat.

Riley shrugged. "We won't know for sure until the blood work comes back, but it looks that way."

"She was conveniently in town for all of this," I said with more than a little glee.

"So it's just a coincidence she knew Rex?" Riley asked. "I don't like coincidences."

I thought about that for a moment. "I don't think Rex is involved. But I do wonder if she and Bobb are working together."

"That's possible, I guess. But I don't know. Bobb's an excellent shot. Why didn't he do all the shooting?"

I shook my head. "No idea. That doesn't really make sense."

"Neither does the fact that they both seemed to be looking for your cat." Riley scratched under Philby's chin, and the cat went limp.

"You killed him!" I wiggled the cat's head, trying to get it to regain consciousness. "Bobb!" I shouted.

Philby hissed himself awake and looked at us like he was ready to tear our heads off.

"B-O-B-B certainly has a connection to your cat," Riley said. He scratched Philby's chin again, and the cat once again passed out.

"It's like those fainting goats. Too much stimulus and they lose consciousness." I said. The cat was still breathing. He just wasn't awake.

"Weird." Riley examined Philby's chin. "I wonder what the guy who can't be named wants with him?"

"You know, even though we've nailed the hoodie shooter, we're still no closer to the truth." My head hurt. Probably from all the wine. "Why don't we call it a night?" I stood up and stretched.

Riley was still staring at the cat. "Okay. Mind if Philby crashes with me tonight?"

"Why? Do you think I can't protect my own cat?" I asked a little defensively. Okay. A lot defensively. It also bothered me a little that he didn't want *me* to crash with him. But then, I was tired. Sex is always better when you're rested.

"No. It's not that." Riley scratched between the sleeping cat's ears. "I just think maybe if I spend a little time with him I could figure all this out."

"Whatever," I yawned. "See you two in the morning. Don't stay up too late."

I got ready for bed and climbed between the sheets. My brain was pulsing with questions. If I've learned anything from years of spying, it's that you can't think on a busy brain. Also, you can't think on an empty stomach, a train ride through India, or when you are drinking absinthe in Paris.

I'd wanted to talk to Riley about all this kissing and worrying about me stuff. I needed to know what it all meant. But did I *want* to know? What would he say anyway? Maybe he was just toying with me?

No, it didn't seem like that. And he was having trouble with the case—losing the guy he was chasing, forgetting stuff he should remember. I'd seen this before. When spies got personally involved, the case always suffered. You couldn't focus on an assignment when you were romantically involved with the person next to you. Instead of the mission coming first, the well-being of your partner came first. It wasn't a good combination.

Riley had been the agency representative sent when the shit hit the fan with me recently. Did they send him, or had he volunteered because he cared about me? I shuddered just thinking about it. If Riley was interested…when did he first feel that way? Had I been blind to it all those years we worked together? Or was it new?

Was he confusing things? Did he just miss working with me and translated that into an affection for me? My head was splitting now. Riley could have feelings for me. Wow. Just…wow.

So why didn't I talk to him about it? That's what you did—you worked through things that jeopardized the mission. And yet, I was afraid to broach the subject. It was possible I was reading this all wrong.

Uh, yeah, I was misreading the kiss. That was the kiss a man gives when he's into a woman. There was no misunderstanding that. Obviously, Riley had a thing for me. When this had all started up, months ago, I'd thought my former boss was acting like this to get me to comply with his orders and agree to his involvement.

It didn't seem like that was the case this time. I wanted him here for extra protection for Philby…to keep the press away when Lenny Smith had showed up dead on my doorstep…but did I want him here also for something else?

Clearly, my body was interested. No wait, I couldn't totally blame my body on this one. I kissed him back. I liked it. No…I'd loved it. So what did it all mean?

Oh, for crying out loud! Now my life was even more complicated. Two men were interested in me. Well, I assumed Rex was still interested in me, and since I didn't know for sure, I was going to believe it.

Two men. I did not need two men fighting over me. Okay—I wanted two men fighting over me a little. But that was bad. I should be more adult about this. Bad, bad, bad.

So what was the answer? Rex or Riley? I hadn't talked to either of them. I'd been avoiding the very subject I wanted answers on. I let that thought stick in my head for a moment.

This was not the way to handle this. I needed to ask Rex what was really going on with our relationship. That was the mature thing to do. And I needed to ask Riley what he was thinking. And I needed to choose between the two.

But who would it be? I fell asleep, wondering.

* * *

I woke up at 11:00 the next morning. Clearly I'd needed rest. Riley's door was still closed. I very carefully opened it to see him and Philby snuggled up forehead to forehead. That had to be a real meeting of the minds. After taking a few pics with my spy camera I let them be, and after taking a shower, I poured a bowl of Lucky Charms, threw in some chocolate chips, and chased it with a Diet Coke. What?

My cell rang. "Hi Dad," I answered with a mouthful of sugar.

"Hey Pumpkin! I've got some orders for you."

My dad had done really well. He'd sold over 400 boxes, and the names on the list read like a political *Who's Who*.

"And your mom wants some shortbread," he finished.

"How is Mom?" I asked, knowing she was fine and fabulous as usual. Geneva Czrygy was a force to be reckoned with. Beautiful and smart, I'd always felt her talents were wasted on DC society. But then, what did I know?

"She's at a Red Cross fundraiser right now. She sends her love," Dad said as we finished the call. I transferred the orders to the forms the Council had given, wondering if they'd believe that the White House Chief of Staff really ordered 100 boxes of lemon cookies.

Because of this, I was feeling better and a bit sugar-buzzed half an hour later when the doorbell rang. It had to be Kelly, I imagined, convinced she wanted to read me the riot act about the night before.

But no, it was Rex darkening my stoop. He wasn't in a suit. Must be the weekend.

"Is it Saturday?" I asked as I opened the door.

Rex looked at me funny. "Strange way to answer the door, but yes. It is Saturday."

"Oh. Okay. Come in," I said. How was I missing what day it was? I didn't have a normal job...or any job...that must be it.

"Actually, I just stopped by to see if you're free tonight."

I frowned, "Do you have another ex-girlfriend you want me to meet?"

"No." Rex scowled. "I can't even get Angela to return my calls today."

I didn't feel bad about that. But it occurred to me that at some point, I'd have to give him the bad news. I'd have to make an effort to do it without skipping and screaming *Yay!* over and over.

"I was going to see if you wanted to come to my house for dinner. I think we need to talk."

And just like that, my mood crashed to the floor. I haven't had a lot of experience dating. But I'd watched enough Dr. Phil in the last year to know that "we need to talk" is bad.

CHAPTER TWENTY-ONE

———

I went back to my Lucky Charms, but my heart wasn't in it. Riley joined me in the kitchen, setting Philby on the counter.

"You're eating that?" he asked, pointing to the sugary goodness.

"I'll have you know, it's got multivitamins in it and is part of a complete breakfast." I shoved the bowl aside. Philby walked over and started to lap up the rainbow colored milk.

Riley made some toast with jelly and joined me. "I think I know what the secret is with this cat."

"What secret?" I asked.

"What B-O-B-B wants with him," Riley said.

Philby looked up at him suspiciously. I was beginning to think he could spell. But the cat just lowered his face and was back at the milk.

"What does he want?" I was starting to sound like a broken record.

"We both talked about this but must've forgotten. Remember that Dr. Rye scanned him for a microchip?" Riley pointed to the back of Philby's neck. Philby ignored him.

"But he didn't find one," I said.

"Right. But just before he didn't find one, he said he felt something strange."

I nodded. "He said it was a fatty tumor or something."

Riley put his fingertips on the back of Philby's neck and rolled a bit of skin between his thumb and fingers. "Feel this." Philby didn't seem to notice.

I did as asked, and I did feel something. "Oh, wow. It's a mini SD card! Like the one in my spy camera!"

Riley looked at me. "I didn't even know you knew about those. You'd always given me the camera."

"I tried to have some photos made at Walgreens with it the other day..."

"You what?" Riley's voice was loud. I didn't like it. "You showed someone a sensitive, covert piece of technology?"

"Forget it," I waved him off. "The girl there was possibly lobotomized as a child. She had no clue."

"I really need you to turn that in." Riley held out his hand.

"Turn what in?" I feigned innocence.

"The camera," he snarled.

"What camera?" I batted my eyelashes like Angela had at dinner. It seemed to work for her.

"I'll get it later. Stop distracting me." He pointed at the cat again. "I think Lenny put something in your cat's neck. Something with state secrets. That's what Bobb wants."

Philby hissed violently at us, spraying multi-colored milk everywhere.

"I can never have a friend with that name now," I sighed.

"So do you think Kelly can do it?" Riley asked.

I froze and stared at him. "You want Kelly to operate on my cat? No way! She can stitch up comatose bimbos any time, but I won't let her cut into my pet!"

Riley scratched his head. "I was hoping to avoid Dr. Rye finding out."

"You don't have a CIA veterinarian?" I asked. "We've had issues involving animals before. Remember that weird goose that ate the microfiche in Honduras?"

"We didn't use a vet for that." Riley glared. "We killed and ate the goose, if you can remember."

"Oh, yeah," I said, staring off into space. "It was pretty good too."

"I don't want to take Philby to DC. We're running out of time. Maybe if we can look at the intel, we can figure out what's going on." Riley said.

"So we do have a CIA vet?" I asked. I'd always wondered. Maybe Lupe the goose didn't have to die.

Riley dialed his cell. "That's classified. I'm calling Rye. Maybe he can see us today."

After he talked to the vet, Riley called Suzanne to bring her up to speed. I heard her ask about the SD card, and Riley told her we wouldn't need the safe house any more. She could go back to her usual business, something I was sure she was grateful for.

My cell rang. "What's up?" I asked Kelly.

"We have a cookie booth sale today," she said. After I said nothing for a moment, she added, "You forgot again. Didn't you?"

I really needed to get a calendar. "No! I knew it was today!"

"I'm waiting for you at the curb."

I hung up and let Riley know I had something to do. He told me Dr. Rye could see us in the afternoon, so I had some time.

I left Riley with Philby and went out to meet Kelly.

As we pulled up to the grocery store, I knew we were in trouble. The pinched, hostile face of Juliette Dowd greeted us. She was pacing beside the six-foot table the store had set up, angrily punching her clipboard with a closed fist. What had I done to piss this woman off?

"Something wrong?" I asked as Kelly unloaded the cases of cookies and the girls started to arrive. We had six girls (and no Kaitlins) signed up for the booth, and they all arrived in two minivans.

She stabbed a finger in my direction. "I don't like you, Ms. Wrath. I don't think you're an appropriate role model for these girls." I wondered if she was a robot who only had those two things to say. Couldn't she come up with something better?

I shrugged. "That's too bad. Because they love me." I wasn't going to screw around with this bitch. Life was too short. Sometimes, people just didn't like you, and that's that. Some folks couldn't handle it. I could, because being liked by everyone didn't matter to me.

"What's going on here?" Kelly muscled her way into the conversation. "What's your problem, Ms. Dowd? Are we doing something wrong?"

Okay, except for the fact that Kelly wanted people to like me.

"I don't have any problem with you." She pointed at my best friend. "But I do question your judgment in choosing this woman as your co-leader." The redhead was practically spitting.

"You're not nice, and I don't like you!" Little Ava was standing between me and Dowd. It was so cute how she defended me.

"You're behaving badly, Ms. Dowd," Kelly snarled. "I really hope you don't end up in my emergency room when I'm working there."

My jaw dropped open. Well at least Kelly was angry at someone else besides me. Once again I wished my best friend had been in the field with me. Especially when I was surrounded by four Muay Thai fighters in a Bangkok alley. If I hadn't had a gun, I wouldn't have gotten out of there alive.

Juliette Dowd viciously snapped her pen into the clipboard. "According to section seven, article five, I can demand that you hold a meeting so I can place you under special observation. You have to set the meeting for tomorrow after school."

Special observation? I didn't like the sound of that.

"Call the parents and make sure your girls will be there. And have an official activity. I'll be watching you, Wrath!"

She stormed over to a green sedan, got in, and peeled out of the parking lot.

"What the hell did you do to that woman?" Kelly asked.

"Yeah!" Tiny Ava glared in the direction of the car. "What the hell?"

Kelly blanched and pushed Ava over toward the other girls, who were putting on their dancing cookie costumes.

"I like that kid," I said. "She's a tough cookie."

Kelly groaned, and the booth sale started as shoppers began wandering in. I didn't have time to wonder about the strange Council administrator who hated my guts. People were buying cookies like they were the last batch on earth. It probably helped that the girls were adorable in their little costumes. Or maybe these cookies were more addicting than heroin. Whatever the reason, we racked up the big bucks and emptied out Kelly's trunk in less than an hour.

"Ice cream on me!" I shouted to the girls when we were done.

A weird old guy grinned toothlessly and walked toward me.

"For my girls only," I amended. The man grumbled an impressive stream of swear words as he walked away. See? It doesn't bother me if someone like him doesn't like me.

"What are you going to do about that woman?" Kelly asked me 10 minutes later as she, I, and six girls slurped ice cream inside a red and white checked store.

I shrugged. "Nothing. She's all talk and no action. I'm not intimidated."

"I know that," Kelly said, one eye on her melting butter brickle cone. "But I don't like it. I think I'm going to report her for harassment."

"Okay." I licked my chocolate fudge brownie ice cream. "I'll help you with the body."

The girls were sticky with ice cream goatees by the time we were done. Their parents picked them up, and Kelly drove me home.

"Wait," she said as I started to open the door. I closed it. "I know I've been a pain in the ass. I don't know what's wrong with me, but it's important to me that you know it's not you."

"Thanks," I said once I wrapped my head around that sentence. "I won't press you for it then. When you're ready to talk about it, I'm here."

Kelly nodded. "I know that. I've got a doctor's appointment in an hour. I'm sure they'll just find that I'm anemic or something. I'll let you know."

I hugged her. "You'd better. Because I need you."

"You do have a lot on your plate right now," she said.

"At least two hunky men who both seem to want me," I blurted out.

Kelly turned off the car. "I've got a few minutes. Spill it."

I told her everything. About dinner with Angela, about my insecurities about my relationship with Rex, and about

Riley's recent kisses. It felt like I was babbling pathetically, but it started to feel good once the last word was out.

"You really do have problems," Kelly sighed. "Granted, they're not bad problems, just inconvenient. But still…what are you going to do?"

I stared at her, "You aren't going to tell me?"

She shook her head. "No. How would I know who you're more interested in? I can't make that decision for you."

"Well, who would you pick?" I asked, hoping this might give me some insight.

"Oh, no." Kelly started the car back up. "I'm not helping you out with this one. You're on your own."

I got out of the car and stuck my tongue out at her. She drove away laughing. At least I knew she and I were good now. That was something, at least.

*　*　*

"There's something there," Dr. Rye announced loudly after 10 minutes of agonizing investigation. I'd been a little late coming back, and when I walked in the door, Riley had Philby under his arm, ready to go.

Philby was trying to sit down on the stainless steel counter top, but failing miserably. He'd definitely put on more weight. His knees, if that's what cats had, wouldn't even bend. Eventually he just sort of collapsed downward, legs splaying in all directions.

"Normally I can just pop that puppy out," Dr. Rye continued. "But this is different. It's a little further in. I'll have to surgically remove it."

"Can you do it today?" I asked. I didn't want to leave Philby here another night because I might go crazy and break in to rescue him again.

Dr. Rye sighed heavily. For a moment I thought he seemed tempted. The vet looked at Riley and me a little longer than was comfortable.

"No. He has to fast for 12 hours. Bring him in the day after tomorrow, first thing in the morning. It won't be too

invasive, and you should be able to take him home that night."
He cocked his head sideways and gave me the once-over.

"After all, I know how hard it is for you to be away from your pet, Ms. Wrath."

"Okay, good," Riley said as he lifted Philby. "See you then, Doc."

We got in the SUV, and Philby sat on my lap, purring.

"We need to be here the whole time," I said. "Once that SD card is out of Philby, we need to have it in our possession."

"I know." Riley reached across and rubbed Philby's ears. "But I don't think the doctor is going to let us be in the surgery with him."

"If that card has sensitive, classified information, we can't let him look at it." I said. "You know the rules."

He nodded. "And if we call it in, the agency will confiscate the cat and do it themselves. Without much regard for Philby's life."

Mrrrrooooooooooooooooooooooooooow! The cat squinted at us.

"Philby doesn't like that idea," I said.

Riley was right. It would be so easy to report everything. But the CIA would probably kill Philby to get what they wanted. There was no way that was going to happen. We'd have to find a way to get the SD card the minute it came out of the cat. But how?

It was late afternoon when we got home. I'd told Rex I'd come over at 5:00. I wasn't looking forward to it. I called to apologize for being so late.

"Sorry, Merry," he said. "I got called into work tonight. Can we do it tomorrow?"

"Sure," I said. "See you tomorrow."

I hung up feeling both relieved and depressed at the same time. Was this better or worse? I just couldn't tell.

Riley ordered takeout from an Indian restaurant I didn't even know existed. It was a quiet night, and we both went to bed with our own thoughts. At least in two days, we'd have that chip out of Philby. Maybe then this whole mess would clear up, and I could move on with my life.

Which would be nice because right now, I had a former boss who'd kissed me, a boyfriend who'd lost interest, a mystery I couldn't begin to wrap my head around, a cranky cat with a strange piece of technical equipment embedded inside him, a best friend with problems of her own, and a woman from the Scout Council who wouldn't be happy until she could roast my body over an open campfire.

The sooner this was all over, the better.

CHAPTER TWENTY-TWO

———

The next day was basically a waiting game for Philby, so I spent the morning preparing for our *mandatory* scout meeting under special observation. I tried to find a project that would be Council approved that didn't have to do with cookies. I was getting a little tired of cookies, and sugaring up the girls wouldn't make anything better.

Kelly and I had decided that if we had to do a special meeting, we might as well work on a merit badge to look good. How bad could it get if we were following the Scout curriculum? Kelly had called the parents the night before, and they were only too happy to let us keep the girls after school for an hour and a half the next day. Kelly said they sounded tired. I could only imagine. One meeting a week was exhausting for me. These people had their kids the rest of the time. I had one cat and needed a nap.

So the next day, I met Kelly at the school. We signed in for our visitor's passes in the office and met the girls in one of the classrooms. To be honest, I was happy to have a little distraction from everything else going on in my life.

Juliette was already in the room when we got there. I wondered if she'd spent the whole day there, drooling and rubbing her hands with glee in anticipation of returning to the office with my head on a spike. Why did she hate me so much?

The whole thing felt weird. Like when someone's watching you but you can't see them. Except that I could see them. Or rather, her. Juliette stood in the corner of the room, clicking her pen. I was pretty sure I saw a bit of insane glee behind those eyes, but that could just be my paranoia talking.

"Okay, girls!" I clapped my hands to get their attention. "Today, we're working on the *Your Future* badge. What do you think that means?"

Ava's hand shot up, "What we're going to do when we grow up! I'm going to be a flower!"

"Almost right," I said. "But I'm pretty sure you can't be a flower."

"Why not?" the girl pouted.

"Because you're a girl. You could, however, be a florist—someone who sells flowers."

Emily raised her hand. "I'm going to be a princess!"

"Well, good luck with that," I said. "Anyway…"

"You can't be the princess!" Betty shouted. "I'm going to be the princess!"

And explosion of arguing broke out, and I glanced toward the corner. Juliette's lips were curled with glee, and she was frantically writing something on a clipboard. What had I done wrong already?

I held up the three finger sign for silence. The room quieted down.

"I happen to know that there's more than one princess in the world. So any of you who can marry into the inbred foreign royalty is welcome to do so in about 11 years. But for now, we have an activity that will help." I signaled Kelly, who started to pass around large squares of poster board and markers.

I continued, "We're going to break you up into groups of three and four to work on this. Has anyone played the Game of Life?"

Lauren stood up, "Aren't we all playing the Game of Life right now? Isn't doing it with a board game a bit redundant?"

Oh, great. A second grade philosopher. I ignored her.

"How many of you know this game?" I asked. Every girl raised her hand.

"Working in your group, you will turn this poster board into a board for your own game. Each space you draw will represent five years and what you will be doing at that time."

Kelly stepped up and showed them the board from the real game and how it worked. More than a few girls looked confused, which made me wonder what they'd thought we were talking about when I asked if they'd played before.

"You have 20 minutes!" I shouted. "Go!"

Kelly and I wandered around the room, making sure the girls colored on the paper, not on each other. Every few minutes I'd look at Juliette, who lurked in her corner like Nosferatu in that black and white movie. We didn't make any effort to acknowledge her. Hell, if I could get away with snapping her neck, I would have. But it probably would've been a bad example for the girls.

"Mrs. Wrath?" one of the Kaitlins asked. "Why is that mean lady here?" She pointed her tiny finger at the corner as if her loud voice hadn't already alerted the viper woman.

"She's from the Council," I explained. "She just wants to observe us."

The girl squinted, frowning. "Can't you just shoot her?"

Yes, I could shoot her. Children don't always make the most reliable witnesses, so I might get away with it. From the corner, I could feel Dowd's eyes burning into my back.

"I'm not going to shoot anyone…" *At least not today.* "Now get back to work before the time is up."

Kelly slid up to me. "Nice save. Did I notice a bit of hesitation?"

"Was she writing all that down on her clipboard?" I asked without looking at her.

"Yup. But I think you could take her." Kelly grinned.

"You *think* I could take her? I'm offended!"

"Ahem!" came a growl behind us. We turned to face one angry redhead. I guess she'd heard us.

"May I speak to you two ladies out in the hall for a moment?" Juliette's face was as red as her hair.

I gasped. "But we can't leave these children unsupervised! That would be against the rules and could possibly result in a dangerous situation!"

"Fine," the woman growled between her teeth. "How about over there, then?" She walked toward the wall on the opposite side of the room. I shrugged at Kelly, and the two of us followed her.

"You see," she hissed, "this is exactly what I was concerned about!" A purple vein popped out on her forehead. "Did I just hear that girl ask if you could shoot me?"

"All kids talk like that," I said. "They don't mean it."

"Oh, they don't, do they?" Juliette vibrated with fury. "I think you're a terrible role model, and it's going in my report!" She stormed back to her corner and glared at us.

I was starting to realize that this wasn't an isolated incident with her. Most likely, Juliette Dowd acted this way a lot. If that was true, the Council probably ignored her outbursts. So I was safe. Probably. Maybe.

"Time's up!" I called out.

The girls turned around and faced me as they giggled in their groups.

"Who wants to go first?" Kelly asked.

The four Kaitlins raised their hands. Of course they were together. Caitlyn stood up holding the poster board while Kaytlynn stood next to her and started speaking.

"Here's where you graduate high school and marry Zayn from One Direction." She pointed to a square with a bunch of stick figures with heads so hairy they looked like werewolves. What was One Direction? And why did they have hair like that? Was it good to marry this Zayn? Why would you want to marry a werewolf? Fearing the answers, I kept these questions to myself.

"Or a handsome prince!" Kaitlin called from the floor.

Kaytlynn nodded. "Oh right. Or a handsome prince." She pointed at the next square. "Here's where you go to Harvard—the only college in the world." A big red building that looked like their school was sitting on the page.

I didn't correct her comment that Harvard was the only college in the world because everyone knew Kaytlynn's parents were a bit on the *helicoptery* side. She probably thought that she had to go there or leave the family in disgrace. Who was I to question anyone's parenting skills?

"When you're out of college," she said pointing to a square that looked like a gray, smooshed building, "you go live in a castle and start your career as a surgeon or lawyer and have two kids, who also become doctors or lawyers."

Kelly stifled a laugh. But I was more concerned with what was next. Was that a picture of a...

"And here's when you're 30 and get to kill all the people who piss you off." Kaytlynn grinned, pointing at a picture of a bleeding stick figure with red hair.

"Oh—okay! Good job!" I said quickly. "You girls can sit down now, and someone else can go."

Kaytlynn frowned. "But I'm not to 40 years old yet! That's when you die because you're so old."

Kelly lost it and doubled over with laughter. She was no help whatsoever.

"How about you guys?" I pointed at Inez and her group.

Inez and Betty stood up, with Emily holding the poster board.

"They started too late!" Inez said. "You have to start here, in elementary school, where you join Scouts and learn about grenades and ninja throwing stars and stuff."

A roar came from the corner, and Juliette stomped over to me. "I'm writing this all down! Consider yourself officially under investigation!" Her eyes were wild, and she was pointing at me over and over. She kind of resembled a deranged hyena with index fingers and a manicure.

"I'm going back to the Council right now! Wait until they hear about this!"

Kelly and I stared as Juliette Dowd fled the room.

"Mrs. Wrath?" I looked down to see Lauren holding up a poster board covered with drawings of people shooting each other and bleeding as they squirmed in their own gore. "Can we go next?"

CHAPTER TWENTY-THREE

When I got home, I took a shower and changed into a clean blouse and jeans. Riley was like a babysitter who had to watch my kid while I went on a date. Or a breakup. I didn't want to think about the idea that our relationship could end in the next 10 minutes.

"I've got to go over to Rex's," I said to Riley. "He wants to talk to me about something." I grabbed my house keys. "You're on Philby protection until I get back. And make sure he doesn't eat anything—he's supposed to fast."

Philby was already making a beeline for his food dish. Well, by making a beeline, I mean moving very, very slowly, but you get the idea.

Riley scooped up the dish and put it in the cupboard. Philby gave him a shocked look.

Mrrrrrrrrrrrrrooooooooooooooooooooooooooooow! he complained.

"This isn't going to be easy," Riley said as Philby started head-butting his shins. It kind of looked like it hurt.

"Good luck!" I said as I ran out the door.

Once the door slammed shut behind me, I walked as slowly as possible across the street. I was in no hurry to be dumped. *Well, Wrath, this is it. Tonight you'll find out how Rex feels, at least.* Maybe that would help with my decision.

Rex opened the door before I could knock. Once inside, he handed me a glass of white wine, and I followed him into the kitchen. I was not prepared for this. Rex had the kitchen table set for two. Nice china, candles, the works.

"We're not watching a movie in the living room with pizza?" I asked, sitting at the table.

"No we're not." Rex said as he stirred something on the stove that smelled heavenly. At least he was going to make me dinner before dumping me. How sad. But still, better to be dumped in a place that wasn't public. And I could slink across the street after.

"Can I help?" I asked, hoping he'd say no. I didn't want to help. It would be like digging my own grave or building my own gallows.

Rex shook his head. "No, you can't. But it's almost done."

The oven made a dinging sound, and Rex pulled a seven-layer lasagna out of the oven. It wasn't even in a tinfoil pan—it was in a real one. He'd made it from scratch. I didn't know he could cook like this. I watched, fascinated as he poured a red sauce from the pan over the lasagna and popped a loaf of Italian bread into the oven. He was going all out for this.

Rex then hand-grated Parmesan cheese over the lasagna and brought the pan to the table. He even used a trivet. Whoa! The oven dinged again, and he took out the bread, expertly slicing it in two and grating more Parmesan cheese over that before putting it on the table as well.

Rex joined me at the table, and we put our napkins (cloth!) on our laps.

"I didn't know you could cook," I said as he served me a huge slice of lasagna and bread.

He nodded. "I should've done this for you a long time ago. It was what you said to Angela that woke me up."

"What I said to Angela?" I mumbled through a mouthful of the best Italian food I'd ever tasted. "So you're not dumping me?"

Rex stared at me. "No! I can't believe you thought that!" He shook his head. "I've been neglecting you. All these months we'd been seeing each other just one night a week, and sitting here, watching rented movies and eating crap pizza. Then an old friend comes into town, and I take her out someplace nice twice."

"The pizza wasn't all that bad..." Breadcrumbs flew from my lips. What was happening here? He wasn't dumping me? Did he really mean it?

"It wasn't what you deserved. I was treating Angela better than I treated my own girlfriend."

I perked up. "So I *am* your girlfriend?"

He sighed. "See? I didn't even let you know how I felt about you. And when you thought I was inviting you out so you could think Angela and I were dating...well, it all came crashing back."

I stared at him for a moment. I kept eating...I'm not an idiot. Yes, the food was that good.

"You aren't interested in Angela?" I asked once my mouth was empty.

"No. Not in the least. I don't even know why I met her for dinner." Rex scowled, and I felt like my heart was bouncing on a trampoline.

"That was a bad idea," I agreed. "But I didn't want to say anything because I thought maybe I'd gotten it wrong about us."

Rex shook his head. "I'm not good at this, Merry. I should've treated you better. It's just that I really enjoy spending an evening with you here. I spend so much time out in the community with my detective face on all day that with you I can really relax."

I hadn't thought of that. Here I'd been thinking I was second string because I wasn't glamorous or fashion forward or whatever. When it turns out that's what he's wanted all along. Rex felt like he could be himself around me. I couldn't think of a better compliment. How did I get this so wrong?

"But what about her lipstick on your collar?" I asked. It was a legitimate question that I could ask now that I knew my status.

Rex blushed. And it was the most adorable thing I'd ever seen. "Sorry about that. The last time we went out, she tried to give me her hotel room key. I told her I wasn't interested. Inviting you to join us was supposed to show her that I was involved with someone. But it didn't because when I dropped her off, she hit on me. I made it clear I didn't want to see her anymore."

"You did?" I actually stopped eating for a moment.

"I did."

"But then, why were you worried she hadn't returned your calls this morning?" I asked.

"I didn't want to leave things on a bad note. And I really wanted her to understand how I felt about you." He checked his phone. "I still haven't heard back from her."

I changed the subject. "Do you know what we really talked about in the bathroom?"

Rex shook his head. His mouth was full of food, and unlike me, he had manners. So I told him what Angela had said to me.

"She said that? To be careful with me because my heart had been broken?"

I nodded. "Why? Is that not true?"

"Well, she left out that she's the one who broke my heart."

"She's a stone-cold bitch," I said. And possibly literally if she was dead now.

"I'll drink to that." Rex clinked my glass.

I needed to tell him. But things were going so well, I didn't want to blow all this great food and apologizing by saying, *Riley shot your friend, and we hid it from you, and she's probably being interrogated by some kind of CIA Coma Interrogators right now.* It just didn't seem to be the right time.

So I told him other stuff. Like how the video showed what looked like but wasn't me on the prison cam. And how Philby was undergoing surgery tomorrow for an SD card that might have classified secrets. And how we didn't know the connection between Bobb and the cat—only that there was one because Philby hissed when he heard his name.

"Huh." Rex said as he got up to put the food away. "I can't think of anything either. You still haven't found him? I could put out an APB."

I shook my head and started clearing dishes. "It's probably better if you don't get involved."

"But I am involved, Merry. Or at least, I want to be." He pushed me away from the sink and wrapped his arms around me.

I reached up and pulled his face to mine, kissing him firmly on the lips. This was way better than I'd thought. I came over here to get seriously dumped only to find that Rex wanted to apologize and stay with me!

His hands ran up and down my back, spreading little flutters across my skin. My lips searched his, and he responded with a little tongue. This was it! Now we were getting somewhere, I thought as I trailed kisses down his throat and started fiddling with the buttons on his shirt. Rex moaned, and it set my body on fire. Oh yeah, we were moving forward now!

A twinge of guilt smacked my gut as I realized I'd made out with two guys in 24 hours. Geez! Was I a slut or what? Of course when I was kissing Riley, I thought Rex and I were through. But now that I was kissing Rex, Riley and I were through. Well, before we were even anything. And I was going to let him know as soon as I got home.

Stop thinking, you idiot, and enjoy this! I was right. Instead of arguing with myself, I let the pleasure of making out with Rex take over. He wanted me—I knew that through every stroke of his hands on my body. It didn't take a genius to know that I wanted him too. He was the one. I had an answer for Kelly.

Okay, I really needed to stop thinking about Kelly. That was easy because thinking was becoming terribly difficult. Rex moaned softly as his lips trailed down my neck and a surge of electricity left sparks in his wake. Oh, yes. Tonight was the night. And I'd bet his sheets were clean.

It felt like my body was vibrating, which was nice. No, wait, it felt like my butt was vibrating. Was it supposed to do that? That was a little farther than I wanted to go the first time, but...

"Your phone is vibrating," Rex whispered in my ear.

"Let's ignore it." I smothered his lips with mine.

"It's still ringing." Rex pulled back. "Do you think it's Riley?"

"Riley can wait," I said, leaning in again.

"What if it's about Philby?" Rex's words washed over me like frozen water.

I pulled the cell from my pocket. It was Riley.

"What's up?" I asked.

"You sound like you're out of breath. Is something wrong?" Riley's voice sounded concerned.

"I'm fine. I ate too much," I covered, feeling very, very guilty. Now that I'd chosen Rex, I felt like I'd led Riley on.

"It's Philby. You'd better come over here. I called Kelly." Riley hung up.

"Oh, no!" I grabbed my keys from the counter and headed for the door. "Something's wrong!"

"I'm coming with you." Rex was hot on my heels.

There was no time to argue. My cat needed me.

CHAPTER TWENTY-FOUR

———

Kelly arrived when I did with her bag of nurse stuff, and we all walked in at the same time. Riley led us into the kitchen. Philby was lying in the middle of the floor on what looked like my pillow, and it looked like he'd just vomited something huge and slimy.

"Is it a rat?" Did I have rats? I did not need rats on top of everything else.

"It's moving!" Riley said. Philby was on his side, panting. Had the rat been rabid and bit Philby?

Kelly grabbed a dishtowel and wiped it off, and I thought I'd probably just throw that one away. She looked at the rat and started laughing. Rex did too. Riley and I were horrified.

"What is it? What's happening?" I asked.

"It's a kitten. Kelly handed me the bundle in the towel. "Philby's a girl. And a mom."

I looked down at the wet bundle and saw that it was, in fact, not a rat. Riley looked over my shoulder. "Philby's a girl?" I asked.

"That's usually how it works," Kelly said, looking at my cat's rear end. "Oh wait, here comes another one."

"Another one?" I gasped.

Rex stepped around us to help Kelly. Riley was also handed a kitten wrapped in a dishtowel. He did what I did—just stared at it.

"That seems to be it." Kelly patted Philby on the head. "Good job, Mama."

Rex took the two kittens from us and put them against the big cat, who immediately started cleaning them up.

"Kittens?" I was still in a bit of shock.

"That's why she was eating so much and looked so fat," Kelly said.

"I'm going to give Dr. Rye a piece of my mind tomorrow before the surgery!" I growled. "He never told us he was a she! Or that she was pregnant!"

Rex shook his head. "She can't have surgery tomorrow. Philby has to feed these two around the clock for the first couple of weeks. No way they can be without her a whole day. You'll have to reschedule the surgery."

Riley cursed. This wasn't good.

"How do you know so much about cats?" I asked my boyfriend. It was so nice to think the word and apply it to Rex.

He shrugged. "I grew up in the country. We had barn cats."

The two babies snuggled against Philby as she licked them vigorously. One kitten was black and the other all-white. At least it would be easy to tell them apart.

"So I have three cats now?" I asked. "Oh my God. I'm a crazy cat lady."

Rex grinned. "I'll tell you what. When they're eight weeks old, I'll take the black one."

I brightened a little. "Deal. Kelly or Riley? The white one's up for grabs."

Riley shook his head. "No way. I'm out of the country half the time. It wouldn't be fair."

I looked at Kelly expectantly. "Robert's allergic, remember?" She looked like she wanted to say more but changed her mind.

"Okay, so you're taking the white one." I ignored her dirty looks. "But what are we going to do about that SD card? We need that to deal with Bobb."

Philby hissed weakly. The two kittens gave tiny hisses. They were definitely Philby's.

"Couldn't you do it?" Riley asked Kelly.

She looked at Philby for a long moment. "I don't know. I've done minor extractions. But even then, she won't be up for it for at least a week. I don't think we can risk it."

I looked at the clock. It was well after 11:00 at night. No way we could cancel with Dr. Rye. I'd have to call first thing in the morning. Meanwhile, Kelly found a box in my garage and lined it with towels. Very gently, she and Rex put Philby and her babies in there.

"I'm still going to yell at the vet," I said.

"In all fairness, he never told you what she was, and you didn't ask," Riley said. "And maybe she delivered early. Maybe he thought he could still do the surgery."

"Or maybe he just thought she was fat. Like you guys did," Kelly said.

Philby was purring as her now clean kittens snuggled up to eat. Wow. I had a family now! Sure, it consisted of cats but still a family and mine!

Kelly mumbled something about having to talk to Robert about something, so she left. I walked Rex to the door, kissing him on my front stoop and watching until he made it to his house across the street. I was just turning to go inside when something where the base of the stoop met the house glinted in the porch light.

I bent down. It was some sort of folded piece of paper. But it was wedged between the concrete and the siding so well it would be tough to get out.

"Riley!" I shouted through the doorway.

He appeared wearing sweat pants and a T-shirt. Huh. When did he have a chance to change?

"Quiet! Philby and the babies are sleeping!" he whispered.

"Look!" I pointed at the paper.

Riley bent down and tried to pry it out while I went inside to get a flashlight and a flat-tipped screwdriver. I got down in the bushes next to the stoop and shone the flashlight.

"The light must have caught on the staple." I said. "How is it possible we didn't notice this before?"

"We haven't really looked, I guess. Neither did the police." Riley jammed the screwdriver into the tiny gap and tried to pry a bigger gap in the cement.

"The paper's the same color as the siding. I didn't even see it when I was cleaning up Lenny's blood."

"Do you have a mallet? Or a small sledge?" Riley asked.

I ran into the garage and found only a regular claw hammer. It would have to do. We were approaching midnight, and I didn't think we could get a contractor here now. I certainly didn't want to leave it out all night if it was a clue.

Riley hit the screwdriver a few times, hard. A chunk of cement broke and I was able to pull the paper out.

"Get it inside," Riley said quickly, looking around.

I was beyond tired. But there was no way I was going to bed without seeing what this was. Riley locked the door and closed all the curtains as I unfolded the piece of paper on the breakfast bar.

"Do you understand it?" I pointed at the columns of numbers on the green ledger sheet. "It makes no sense to me." There were just strings of five-digit numbers and a couple of times were the letters *LS* and *SS*. What did it mean?

"It's some kind of code." Riley frowned and rubbed his eyes. "It all looks so blurry. I need some sleep."

I nodded. "Let's divide and conquer. I'll take the cats to bed with me. You take the clue."

"Good idea." He kissed me on the forehead. "See you in the morning." And with a wink, he was gone. For a moment I wanted to run down the hall after him and tell him there'd be no more kissing. That I was with Rex and not him. But the door to his room closed, and I had kittens mewing behind me. Tomorrow. I could tell him tomorrow.

I lugged the box to my room and set it on my bed. I decided to sleep in sweats in case I needed to get up. I'd grabbed my gun from the basement earlier and had it on my nightstand. I turned off the light and curled my body around the box. No way anyone was getting to these cats tonight. Philby's purring immediately put me to sleep.

CHAPTER TWENTY-FIVE

———

My alarm woke me up at 8:00 a.m., and I called Dr. Rye immediately. I told him what had happened the night before.

"Pregnant? Well, you're right. We can't operate for a little while then. How are the kittens?" he asked. I toyed with chewing him out for not mentioning Philby being a girl or pregnant but decided against it. I wasn't sure how hard it was to find a vet. Maybe it's like trying to find a doctor who takes your insurance. Or maybe it's worse.

"They look fine, I think," I said as I looked the sleeping kitties over. "I'm really not sure, actually."

"Why don't you bring them in anyway? I can at least do the first checkup, and you'll feel a lot better," Doc said.

"That's a good idea." I was really nervous about this and had a lot of questions. "Same time?"

"Same time," Dr. Rye said. "See you soon."

Riley got up when he heard me speaking and agreed that this was a good idea. We quickly got dressed and wrapped the box in blankets before carrying it to the SUV.

"I'm still shocked that Philby had kittens," Riley said as he drove.

"I'm still shocked that Philby is a girl," I said. I kept checking the kittens every two seconds. "I know how to pick 62 different types of locks. I can dismantle, clean, reassemble, and load any gun in five minutes. I know the names of every terrorist sect and sub-sect in the world. But I know nothing about cats."

"Thank God for Kelly and Rex," Riley said as he pulled into the parking lot. I felt a twinge of guilt at the mention of Rex. But now was not the time to talk to Riley.

We carried the box in and checked in with the receptionist who took us to the exam room.

Dr. Rye burst into the room and handed me a bunch of pamphlets. "About kittens, Ms. Wrath."

He examined Philby and each kitten. He did his usual staring silently for a long time.

"I want to weigh them and check their stool samples. This will take a little while. Why don't you sit in the waiting room?" the doc finally said.

"Is something wrong?" I asked. Please don't let something be wrong...

Dr. Rye smiled and shook his head. "No. Nothing like that. I just want to get their measurements, observe them feeding, all basic stuff. Too many people in here will distract Mama."

Riley put his hand on my shoulder. "Come on, Merry. Let's get this over with." He guided me out the door and down the hall to the lobby, where we sat.

"It shouldn't take too long," I said. "We're the only ones here."

Riley nodded. "Let's take our mind off it by thinking about this." He pulled the ledger page out of his pocket, and we stared at it in hopes something would magically appear and explain it.

"It doesn't look like orders for something," I said, pointing to the columns. "I thought that was it at first, with columns for dates, quantity, etc. But I think it's something else." And by *think*, I meant that I had absolutely no clue.

"These numbers are all five digits long," Riley mused. "Could they be commercial codes?"

"Huh." I took out my cellphone and went to the browser. I typed in the first number and hit search. "That's weird."

Riley looked at my phone. "Wait...try another one."

I typed in another number and the same thing came up.

"No way," I said as we looked at each other.

The receptionist came back to the desk and sat down, startling us. I heard mewing at the end of the hall. How long had it been?

"Dr. Rye's a good vet, right?" I asked her.

The woman looked up at me quizzically. "What?" She was in her early 30s, blonde hair pulled back severely into a bun. Her nametag said *Anna.*

Riley must've been worried too. "We're just a little nervous. These are our first kittens."

"Oh." She frowned like she was thinking of something. "I don't really know. I'm just a temp."

"Okay." I said. "Can I talk to one of the nurses?"

"You mean Vet Assistants? We don't really have nurses." She seemed confused even when correcting us.

"Okay," I said. "One of those. Can we speak to them?"

"You could. If they were here. I'm the only one right now, and I don't really know the others."

Riley and I exchanged looks. "You don't know the other people who work here?"

She shook her head. "It's a really new office."

A chill went through me. "How new exactly?"

The woman shrugged, and I jumped to my feet, running down the hall toward my cat with Riley hot on my heels.

I threw open the door to see Philby, alone and covered in blood, with the kittens mewing loudly from their box. I checked my cat. A savage cut tore across the back of her neck and she was barely breathing.

"My cat!" I cried.

"The chip!" Riley growled as he drew his gun and took off.

I called Kelly, putting her on speaker and tried to bandage my cat's neck.

"Please don't die!" I said over and over as I wrapped her in a blanket to keep her warm. Philby looked at me and laid her head back down.

"Who's dying?" Kelly's voice asked.

I told her what had happened, and she said she'd meet me at a veterinarian's office about five minutes away.

The receptionist wandered in, and I demanded she grab the box of kittens and follow me. Riley was nowhere to be found, but because he'd carried the cats' box, I'd had his keys.

I've driven in some bad circumstances before. The worst had to be the Death Road in Ecuador—a muddy, barely single lane road that crumbled over a horrible chasm—while being chased by drug runners shooting AK-47s in my direction. At night.

This was worse. It was rush hour, and I wasn't totally sure where the vet's office was or if they were open. Philby's breathing was growing shallow and the kittens were protesting loudly. I swerved to the right roughly, apologizing to the cats, and came to a screeching stop outside a building with a huge plastic parrot over the door.

Was it just a bird doctor? What kind of vets just did birds? *Well, birds are just cats with feathers, right?* I thought frantically as I grabbed the box and ran for the door. It was unlocked. The waiting room was full of people with various animals, but I ran up to the counter and showed Philby to them.

"Come on back!" A woman dressed in scrubs insisted, and I followed her. She set me up in a room, and a tall, thin, middle-aged woman came in seconds later. She had a kind face, which was good, or I would've shot her.

"I'm Dr. Glen," she said without looking at me, because she was examining the cat. "Someone cut her open," Dr. Glen said. "She's lost a lot of blood."

I told her everything while she gave Philby a shot and nodded occasionally. Kelly burst into the room and stood there, staring at the mess.

"Dr. Rye has been on medical leave for two weeks," the vet said. "His practice was supposed to be closed except for boarded animals."

Kelly's jaw dropped open.

"I just figured that out," I said sadly. How could we have been so stupid? And yes, I was including Riley in the *we*. See how bad it is when a couple works together? We were *so* over. And his concern for the chip instead of Philby? Oh yes. This talk was going to be easier than I thought.

Finally the vet looked at me. "Go to the waiting room. I need to get some more of my staff in here to help."

Kelly snatched the box of kittens and we went back to the lobby.

"Too many people," I said, and she nodded, following me out to the SUV. I ran the engine to keep the kittens warm and took a deep breath.

"What the hell happened?" Kelly shouted. "Where's Riley? Who did this to Philby?"

"The fake Dr. Rye did this to my cat," I said, holding back my anger. "Riley should be shooting him in the balls about right now. If not, then I'll be shooting him in the balls later."

I should've known something was off when Rye didn't tell me the cat was female and pregnant. I was seriously losing my touch. Things were starting to come together in my mind, but I didn't have it all figured out yet. I needed Riley to put the last few pieces together.

"Who is the fake Dr. Rye?" Kelly asked.

I shook my head. "I don't know, but he's not a vet. In fact, I'm pretty sure he's a spy."

"So Angela's a spy, and the vet is a spy, and Bobb is a spy?" Kelly asked while Philby's tiny progeny hissed in unison.

"No, Angela's not of the same caliber. I think she and Bobb work for the same person, and all of this ties in to the beginning with Lenny Smith showing up to die on my stoop." The kittens hissed more weakly this time. I'm sure they were hungry.

"And Midori?" Kelly was stroking the kittens. "Could this have to do with her?"

"I've no idea." Bits and pieces of the puzzle were filled in, but not the whole picture.

My cell buzzed, and I read the text.

"Riley wants me to meet him at the safe house," I frowned. "I can't leave Philby and the kittens."

Kelly opened the door to the car and got out with the box. "Go. I've got this."

I hesitated but another text came through. All it said was, *Hurry Finn!!*

"All right." I said as I put on my seat belt. "Let me know the minute you talk to Dr. Glen."

Kelly nodded and took the box back into the vet's. I pulled out of the parking lot and onto the street. I would go meet Riley, but first, I was going to stop at my house and get my gun.

CHAPTER TWENTY-SIX

"Are you sure about this?" Rex asked as he climbed into the car wearing his body armor and packing his service pistol.

I nodded. "You called in reinforcements?"

"I did. They'll be there. It was tough to explain why I needed a yarn shop surrounded, but they'll do it. What made you so certain something was up?"

Throwing the car in reverse, I gave him a look. "Riley called me Finn. He doesn't call me Finn. Not since before I moved here."

It had been inspired, really. Either Riley texted that to warn me, or someone had his phone and didn't know I went by Merry now, but it didn't matter. Something was wrong, and I had to deal with it.

As I drove, I filled Rex in on what had happened to Philby.

"Bastard," Rex growled. "I hate people who prey on helpless animals."

"And there's something else you should know." I bit my lip and gave him a weak smile. "It's about Angela."

"What about Angela?" He asked.

"Well, she's in a CIA holding area after Riley shot her for shooting at us." Okay, that could've come out better, but a little old lady dodged into the road, and I had to swerve to miss her.

"What?" Rex shouted. I told him everything. There was no point in holding back now. He listened in silence, and when I was done, shook his head.

"Wow. Just...wow. What is it with all of my exes being crazy?"

"Wait…all of your exes? As in more than one?" I asked. And did he say they'd all been crazy?

"Watch where you're going!" Rex grabbed the wheel to steer me out of the way of an oncoming truck.

A minute later, I slammed on the brakes. We were a block away at a shop across the street from All About Ewe. I didn't want to just walk into an ambush. Rex led me into the furniture store, and we went to the back room to check the windows.

"I don't see anything unusual." Rex frowned.

"I do," I said as I checked my gun. "The sign says *Closed* in the middle of the day."

My boyfriend, the cop, sighed. "So, what's the plan?"

I shrugged. "Time to go in. Just me. Alone."

Rex shook his head. "Oh no. I'm going with you."

"You can't. You're the cavalry. If I don't come out in five minutes, you and your guys come in."

"No. I don't like it," he said.

"I'll be fine." I kissed him. "But make sure you come in and rescue me."

"You have two minutes. Not five." Rex kissed me back. "Starting now."

I walked out of the furniture store, around the corner and right up to All About Ewe. The lights were out inside. My fingers gripped the door handle for a moment, and I felt the confidence of my pistol in my waistband. With a deep breath, I pulled open the door and went in.

"Hello? Suzanne? Riley?" I called out trying to sound like I didn't suspect anything. No one answered. I found the lights and switched them on and still didn't see anyone. Whoever it was who'd wanted me there must be in the safe house in back.

As I walked through the store, I picked up a pair of wooden knitting needles that had wickedly sharp points and shoved them into my back pocket. There was no sound as I approached the bookcase that hid the door. I shoved it aside and slowly opened the door. It was dark.

A bullet hit the doorframe less than a centimeter from my head. I drew my gun as I dropped and fired in the direction the shot came from. A man cried out in pain, and I silently prayed it wasn't Riley as I rolled across the floor to where I'd remembered the bed being.

"*Aaaaaaaaaaaaaaaaarrrrrrrrrrrrrrrrgh!*" A woman's scream thundered toward me, and I put my arms up in time to catch her before she dropped on top of me. Hands that felt like a steel vice circled my throat and squeezed. I brought my arms up between hers and down over them to break the grip, then brought my knees up hard, knocking her headfirst into the wall behind me. Her body shuddered before going limp.

Another shot rang out, a little to my left. I started crawling to my right, trying to focus in the dim light. It was hopeless. I didn't want to shoot without knowing if Riley was in here. I kept going until my head smacked on the table.

Stars filled my vision, and I dropped to the floor just as someone lunged on top of me and used his knee to crush my throat. It was working. I felt all over the leg until I felt blood. My first shot must've gone through his thigh. I jammed my finger into the wound.

My assailant screamed but kept pushing his knee into my neck. Even though I struggled, I felt consciousness slipping away. I couldn't breathe at all, and in a second my trachea would be crushed.

I fought through the encroaching darkness and pain, feeling my attacker's breath on my face. Fighting was no use, and I remembered I had another weapon. Reaching back to my pocket, I pulled the knitting needles out and jabbed upward as far as I could reach.

A scream brought me back to life as the knee lifted off my throat. I gasped for air and scrambled to my feet as light flooded the room and Rex, followed by four uniformed policemen, ran in.

Suzanne was crumpled against the wall where I'd left her. Bobb was gurgling as he clawed at two knitting needles plunged into his throat, his thigh bleeding heavily from the gunshot wound. But Dr. Rye and Riley were nowhere to be found.

"I remember this guy," Rex said 10 minutes later as paramedics were loading Bobb onto a gurney. "But who is that?" He pointed to Suzanne's dead body that lay where it fell. Apparently, slamming into the wall had snapped her neck. Too bad.

"Suzanne Smith," I said as I rubbed my throat.

"Like Lenny Smith?" Rex asked.

I nodded. "His daughter. When Daddy was arrested, she changed her name and joined the CIA. Turns out, she was the mastermind spy. Not her father. He just took the heat for her."

Rex stared at me. "You didn't tell me about her."

I shrugged. "Because she didn't register. She was invisible. Unnoticeable and had been vetted by the agency as Suzanne Aubrey."

"I still don't know how you figured that out," Rex said.

"Remember how I told you I'd found that ledger sheet? Riley and I didn't get it at first. But then I googled a little bit of it on my cell while waiting at fake Dr. Rye's. What popped up was a newspaper article about a young girl who'd won the Westinghouse Award for writing computer code. The girl was Suzanne. And in the background was the photo of her parents, Ann and Lenny Smith." I'd seen their initials on the sheet, *SS* and *LS*.

Rex shook his head. "I don't get why the internet address for an old news article would be on a ledger sheet?"

"I'm not entirely sure. But I'd guess that Lenny was seeking me out because he wanted to tell me that his daughter was responsible for the espionage he'd been imprisoned for."

"Why would he turn on his daughter if he took the rap for her in the beginning?" Rex asked.

"I don't know. Maybe they'd become estranged? Maybe she didn't send him a card on Father's Day? Who knows?" I shrugged.

"But that doesn't explain Angela, Bobb, the chip in Philby's neck, Dr. Rye, or why Riley disappeared. There's too much we don't know," Rex said.

"Fortunately, it's not your problem." I nodded and pointed at the door. Two older CIA agents had entered the room and were taking control of the situation. They flashed their ID at us.

Rex sighed. "Okay. But will you come by later and fill me in?" He kissed me before gathering up his men and joining the two agents.

I sat down on the bed and checked my cell.

Philby's going to be fine. Kelly texted. *Bringing her and the kittens back to my house after they finish stitching her up.*

Closing my eyes, I leaned back against the wall. At least they were safe. Now I just needed to find Riley. Hopefully, he had Dr. Rye's head in a bag for me to punch.

"Good job, Ms. Wrath." One of the CIA suits was standing in front of me when I opened my eyes. "I can see we lost a good agent with you."

I stood. "Thanks. And you are?"

He held out his hand. "Chuck Winslow." He motioned to his partner. "And this is Dennis Gray."

I shook their hands and didn't ask any more questions. I recognized the faces and names. They'd worked with Cy Stern on the Lenny Smith case.

"I have to ask," I ventured. "Why did Lenny come see me when he got out? I never worked with him."

Dennis Gray answered. "The woman who impersonated you at the prison visit gave him your name and told him where to find you. Her partner, the man you called Bobb, broke him out and got him here. They worked for the daughter." He pointed at the dead woman.

"They thought he might give you the information on the missing SD card, since you weren't an active agent anymore," Winslow finished. "They didn't think he'd betray Suzanne in the process. Once they realized that, they killed him."

Of course these two knew everything. And of course they never thought that was important enough to tell Riley. The CIA worked in mysterious ways. Agents never trusted anyone but their partner. Asking these two why they'd let things get so out of hand was worthless. They wouldn't tell me anyway.

"So Lenny had microchipped his cat, but with the SD card instead," I said.

The men nodded. "That's what we think too. But it wasn't his cat. It was just a stray he'd found and took in to some vet on his way here. Bobb followed him after busting him out of Florence. He knew the cat was important but didn't know how."

"So do you guys know how Lenny escaped from a supermax prison?" I asked.

"That's classified, Ms. Wrath," they said in perfect unison.

I excused myself and drove the SUV home. Kelly called to say she'd take care of Philby and the kittens overnight. I was so tired, I agreed. I cleared the house before going to the kitchen and pouring a glass of wine. Where was Riley? And where was fake Dr. Rye?

CHAPTER TWENTY-SEVEN

My cell phone rang, jolting me awake. I'd fallen asleep on the couch with my gun on my stomach. Not good form.

"Riley?" I asked as I checked the caller ID. "Where are you?"

"Sorry, Merry. I can't say," Riley answered apologetically.

"Ah," I said, slumping back onto the couch. "It's classified, right?"

"Yes. I'm chasing Rye, if that helps," he said.

"He's not part of the Smith situation then, is he?"

"Not really, except for the secrets Smith stole. But it does have to do with an earlier problem. Have some sushi, and I'll check in later." He hung up.

Kelly rang my doorbell first thing in the morning. I was so happy to get Philby and the kittens back that I didn't mind that it was 6:00 a.m.

"Dr. Glen says they'll all be just fine." Kelly smiled as she stroked Philby's cheek.

My cat looked like a deflated basketball with a Frankenstein scar and stitches across her shaved neck. Cool. This would take the embarrassment away from looking like Hitler.

"Sure you don't want one of the kittens?" I asked as I set the box on the couch between us.

Kelly shook her head. "No, I'd better not."

"Because of Robert's allergies?" I asked. "Hey, by the way, I'm sorry I didn't ask how your doctor's appointment went. What did they say is wrong with you?"

"Well," Kelly said slowly. "I've got a parasite condition."

"What? That's horrible! Like a tapeworm?" That made sense. Stuff like that often made you tired because the parasite devoured all your nutrients.

"It's worse than that, actually." Kelly frowned.

Oh, crap. "Must be some big parasite." I looked around her to see if she had a lamprey on her back or something— although I was pretty sure I wouldn't have missed something like that.

Kelly sighed heavily. "It is a big parasite. I'm pregnant."

The next day, I was at Rex's house, snuggled on the couch with my cat family. In spite of my previous ambitions of going out to someplace nice, it seemed better to stay home with my boyfriend, my badass mama cat, and two little kittens.

"There's just one thing I don't understand," Rex asked as the kittens slept soundly on his chest. "What did the fake vet want the SD card for if he wasn't involved with the Lenny Smith case?"

I shook my head. Rex didn't know about Midori, and I wasn't ready to tell him about it until I knew more. "I guess there was some sort of intelligence Smith had hidden on there that had to do with something else."

"It's very confusing," he said, petting the purring kittens. "Even for a detective."

I kissed him very slowly. "It's very confusing for an ex-CIA agent too. Half the time though, cases are intertwined like this. My guess is that another interested party was looking for some info Lenny had promised to the Chinese but never delivered. Suzanne just wanted to recover any intel that was still out there. We may never know what was on that SD card, even when Riley recovers it, because the brass at the agency will take it."

I suspected that it had to do with technology secrets that the Yakuza had wanted as well. But there was no point speculating until I knew more.

"How did Riley's phone text you if he wasn't there?"

I sighed. "Suzanne hacked it somehow. Riley has his phone, but she hijacked the technology."

"I'm still surprised about Angela. I didn't see that coming," Rex said.

"Suzanne recruited her because she had a connection here. Suzanne wasn't really from WT. She wanted someone who knew the layout of town. Angela took the gig with no experience because she thought she'd get to take me out and regain you." I didn't tell Rex that I knew this from Angela's interrogation once she came out of the coma. And he didn't ask.

"What surprised me was that Bobb wasn't *the* Bobb," I said in an attempt to change the subject.

Philby raised her head and stared at me for a moment. She didn't hiss. She just stretched her paws and laid back down closing her eyes. Bobb hadn't made it to the emergency room. He'd died on the way. I'd managed to kill two people in one night—a new and unseemly record for me. I think Philby knew that.

The CIA identified Bobb as a two-bit hustler who just took on the real assassin's persona thinking it made him seem more badass. Suzanne hadn't been very careful in recruiting henchmen. But we'd never be able to ask her. And I didn't mind a bit.

"You said something I've been meaning to ask you about," I said. "Something about all your exes being crazy?"

Rex nodded. "Yeah. I've only had two. Angela was the second. The first one was in high school and a real psycho. Extremely jealous. She practically ruined the lives of any girl I even talked to. I really hope you never have to meet *her*."

"She sounds awful. Not nearly as cool and awesome as your current girlfriend." I said.

The doorbell rang. Rex and I exchanged looks as he set the kittens down on the couch and checked the peephole. He relaxed and opened the door.

Twenty-four second grade girls poured into the room, followed by Kelly. They swarmed me and the kittens, a loud *awwwww!* rattling the house.

Rex stepped in and scooped up the kittens, talking to the girls about them as they crowded around him.

"They really wanted to see them," Kelly said.

"You had no choice," I replied as I stood next to her and watched.

"This is the second time you've had one of your hotties work with the girls," Kelly whispered. "What will they think of you?"

"You're right. I need to talk to Riley," I said quietly so Rex wouldn't hear. Not that he could've heard over the din of squealing Girl Scouts.

"So no more making out with your former boss?" Kelly asked.

I shook my head. "I can't date two guys at once." Rex was the winner. He was here, he could cook, and he made my heart race. Riley was gone half the time and too much of a player. I didn't look forward to telling him this. But I was making the right decision.

"What were you two doing when we interrupted?" Kelly arched one eyebrow.

"Just talking about Rex's hostile ex-girlfriends. Right, Babe?"

Rex laughed. "That's right. But the one from high school was a nightmare. Even with your background, Merry, I wouldn't want you to meet her."

Kelly asked, "You grew up around here, didn't you? Who was she?" She gave me a wink, and I giggled. If she was worse than Angela, I was totally steering clear of this woman.

"A redhead," Rex said as he held one of the kittens out for the girls to coo over. "She works for the Scout Council, I think. Her name is Juliette Dowd."

ABOUT THE AUTHOR

Leslie Langtry is the author of the *Greatest Hits Mysteries* series, *Sex, Lies, & Family Vacations*, *The Hanging Tree Tales* as Max Deimos, the *Merry Wrath Mysteries*, and several books she hasn't finished yet, because she's very lazy.

Leslie loves puppies and cake (but she will not share her cake with puppies) and thinks praying mantids make everything better. She lives with her family and assorted animals in the Midwest, where she is currently working on her next book and trying to learn to play the ukulele.

To learn more about Leslie, visit her online at www.leslielangtry.com

Enjoyed this book? Check out these other fun reads available in print now from Gemma Halliday Publishing:

www.GemmaHallidayPublishing.com

79612531R00109

Made in the USA
Columbia, SC
05 November 2017